# Pink Lies in Paris

## - a novel -

### Haley Todd Kitts

Set in New York City, New York
Paris, France
Various places in Europe
Charleston, South Carolina

LIBRARY OF CONGRESS CATALOGING-PUBLICATION-DATA
Names: Kitts, Haley Todd
Title: Pink Lies in Paris: a novel/ Haley Todd Kitts

ISBN: 9781521790403

*Edited by: Laci Swann; Sharp Editorial*
*Cover & Illustrations by Victoria Blanchard*
*Graphic Design by Jayce Williams*
*Formatted by Shannon Passmore, Shanoff Formats*

# Table of Contents

*For my husband, Marcus, who asked me to*
*move to France with him back in 2013.*
*That's where our love story truly began!*

For Jackie
& Haley

# One

## je t'aime

As you know by now, I have a terrible time organizing for a major trip. At least I have a much larger closet since moving in with Hugh. My grand-parents aren't thrilled with the idea of me "living in sin," but they should be happy I'm trying to be practical. I'll never get ahead in this city unless I save every penny. Cabot was actually very understanding when I told her I was moving out. I live in the same building as my boyfriend, so I can't see paying the astronomical price of rent when he's only an elevator ride away. She was able to sublet my room to our friend, Cooper – one of the graphic designers at *Cosmo*. I'm not going to lie –they are a match made in heaven. Cooper appreciates the Kate Spade china more than I ever could.

Packing is literally the bane of my existence. Paris is only three days away, and I have yet to figure out what to bring. With so many events to attend, I'm lucky *Cosmo* gave me a hefty wardrobe allowance or I would be wearing my lime green, sequin prom dress I bought at the Citadel Mall. Not sure I would even fit in that thing now, come to think of it. There are so many times I would rather be a guy; right now is one of those times. Hugh finished all of his laundry and packed his clothes into what I like to call a "thimble." When you don't wear colors, you don't have to pack as much. I've been dating Hugh for months and still can't figure out if he's repeated an outfit yet. My main issue with packing is wanting to take every cute pair of shoes that I own and not being able to decide which are going in the "no" pile. My mother suggested I buy some scarves and black boots so I don't look like a tourist. The truth is – I am, in fact, a tourist; I don't even care. You will find me wearing my Converse and consignment shop clothing on the streets of Paris. I have a thing about being comfortable over being fashionable, which seems like an oxymoron considering I work in the fashion sector of *Cosmopolitan Magazine.*

"Do you think if we went for a walk and came back you could clear your head and focus on packing tonight?" Hugh asked in such a tender, loving way, as he poured chai tea into my favorite mug which reads "#IWokeUp-LikeThis" in bold, black font.

"I don't think you understand," I said while taking slow sips of my warm, cardamom drink hoping he will just *let it go.* "I can't focus on anything but getting this done before tomorrow."

"I think it's much like studying for a very important test, my love. You must take a short break to give your brain some rest," Hugh says as he kisses my forehead like he always does when consoling me.

"If it will make you happy to go on a walk, I will… as long as some kind of dessert is involved."

You'd think after drinking sugary tea I wouldn't need a dessert, or the fact that I'm about to live in Paris for the next three months where the pastries are more than abundant. You will probably be able to roll me down a hill after I get back. Hell, I can just smell food and gain weight!

"I think I can make that happen. How about some cupcakes from Magnolia Bakery?" Hugh asks, even though he already knows my answer.

"I can't argue with that," I say with a huge grin on my face.

•••

Once we make it back from our long walk to Magnolia's, I decide it's time to phone a friend – my best friend, Addison. Addison is going into her second semester at Georgetown Law, and she never has time for me anymore. I want her to soak up these last few days of being in the same time zone because once I'm in France she'll never have a chance. I don't think she would appreciate me video chatting her at six in the morning, or one in the morning for that matter. She says she gets a spring break, and she is considering coming to Paris to spend a week with me. Do I think that will happen? Heck no, but it's worth getting excited about.

"Are you and Hugh going to live in a flat with a view of the Eiffel Tower?" Addison asks presumptuously.

"I don't think *Cosmo* wants us shacking up in Paris together. I'm not really sure what our living arrangements will be, but I doubt we will have a ten-million-dollar view," I say, shifting the camera to the window in the living room.

"Don't you think they can afford it? Geez," Addison asks.

"You would think that, wouldn't you?" I reply.

"Absolutely, yeah, I would. Hopefully you will have some time for yourself and won't be working the entire time," Addison responds.

"I know wherever I am in France, as long as I have access to a warm room with Wi-Fi, I'll be a happy girl," I say, holding a cozy Brookstone blanket to my face.

"Amen to that," Addison says while raising her hands up with praise.

After FaceTime with Addison, I decided it was time to buckle down and get everything organized for Paris. I've never been to Europe, but I have been on a trip with my family to Hawaii, which seemed like another country being that it took so long to get there. Not to mention, my mom and sister's luggage was "misplaced" by the airline. They wore the same outfits for three days until their bags finally arrived. That's probably my biggest fear with this trip. If our Hawaii trip taught me anything, it's to pack a few outfits in your carry-on. I will never be unprepared after that little incident occurred with mom and Savannah.

It's hard to know what to pack for a trip that lasts twelve weeks in a foreign country. Hugh has been out of the country for photo shoots several times, so he has this traveling thing down to a science. Not to mention, he's flown from Australia to New York countless times over the years. If I could hire an expert to pack for me, I would. Come to think of it, there are probably people you can hire to pack for you, but it would, no doubt, cost an arm and a leg. It's funny how you can download an app to find a boyfriend, yet you can't download an app to hire someone to pack for you. If only I could "swipe right" to find the perfect person to pack for me. I laid everything on the floor, in the middle of the room, folded neatly, and showed Hugh my progress.

"Look, babe! I'm almost done organizing the plethora of items I need for this trip." I say it like a cute five year old with pleading eyes hoping he won't care that we leave in forty-eight hours and I can't get myself together. "I have almost everything ready to go. I just need to put it in my suitcases."

"I see that, Scarlett. Well done. Now roll those clothes up and put them in the bag, so I can roll around in bed with you until we fall asleep," Hugh commanded in a seducing tone of voice.

Hugh probably patronizes me more than I know, but it's hard to tell with his hot Australian accent. I never get tired of hearing him speak to me. It doesn't matter if he's just asking me to pass the salad dressing at dinner – I just like hearing him speak.

If you would've told me, four years ago, I would be in love with a hot Australian man, I would have laughed hysterically in your face. I seem to fall more in love with this guy each and every day. Of course, he's gorgeous, but he's also generous and kind. He's sweeter to me than anyone on this planet, besides my grandfather, who Hugh can't exactly compete with. It's different.

Speaking of my grandfather, he wants to talk to me before I leave to discuss some *pressing* matters. I'm really hoping these are good, "pressing" matters, and not serious ones. I always worry about him since he's getting older, that he's going to come to me with bad news of his health or something terrible.

Now that all of my clothes are packed away, I guess Hugh will have to endure me walking around the apartment with little to no garments on. What a shame. What guy doesn't want his girlfriend walking around in negligees all night? I haven't met any. Come to think of it, I haven't dated that many guys, so I wouldn't really know. I didn't have time for dating in college because I told myself I would not get serious with anyone until I was old enough to know what I really wanted out of life. I think I'm still figuring that out, but I'm much more content than I was when I was at the College of Charleston. Plus, the guys were a bit too artsy for me. You know when *they* say, "When you find out who you truly are, you can be happy." Well, come to think of it, I think I have finally figured out who Scarlett is – I am a woman who works for the magazine of my *dreams*, I date the hottest guy I have ever laid eyes on, and I'm about to move to Paris for a few months. What could be wrong with that?

•••

"I have some old, silk t-shirts you can borrow until we leave. I think you'll like them because they're really soft. I think I'll like you in them even more," Hugh says while pulling them out of his closet.

"Babe, aren't these like $400 each?! What in the world? How do you have such expensive shirts just lying around?" I ask with my arms crossed at my chest and my eyebrows raised as high as they could go.

"Well, I've never mentioned this for very good reasons, but when I was twenty, I was a model for Saint Laurent back home in Australia. They scouted me when I was trying on clothes in the men's department of this fancy mall in the city," Hugh says while meticulously folding and re-folding the shirts on the bed.

"Are you serious? Oh my gosh! I have to see these photos. I bet you were so hot," I say while hopping off the bed to come feel the silky shirts that were once on the back of young Hugh Hamilton.

"I was young and very skinny. Perfect to model these tight, over-priced t-shirts," Hugh says while holding the shirts to his chest.

"Oh, please! I bet you still look great in them. Why didn't you tell me this? I feel like I learn something new about you every day. I'm not complaining..."

"Well, it just hasn't come up. It's not something I tell unless I have to. I'm not embarrassed by it or anything. I just don't think it's interesting. I was a model, and now I'm not," Hugh says as he tosses the shirts on the bed.

"I still think you could model. You are so hot, babe," I say while tugging on the front of Hugh's jeans to pull him closer to me.

Hugh looks up at me with a smirk on his face, clearly delighted with the response I gave him. "Well, thanks, love. I appreciate how you swoon over me, but I'm not *all that*. I'll have to find those pictures on a hard drive somewhere. I buried them so nobody would haunt me with them later. How about we just change subjects and get you dressed since you clearly insist on it."

Being that it's January and I'm freezing, I decided to keep the silk shirt on at all times to avoid frostbite. Hugh prefers I just go topless for the next couple of days, but even with the heat on it's frigid in here. I think if there was carpet in this place I would feel a lot cozier. Something about this apartment still needs a female touch. Perhaps when we are back from Paris, Hugh will let me pick out some rugs. Maybe by then my feet will be thawed out. I'm still not used to the cold. I don't think I will *ever* get used to the cold. Unfortunately, I'm about to feel the tundra for another few months because Paris won't warm up until we're about to come home. I've only seen significant snowfall a few times in my life. When I say significant, I mean ten inches *at best*. That's not even enough snow to make a decent snowman or miss school for several days. Well, I take that back. In Charleston, I believe they shut everything down for a mere dusting. I've been sledding once, and the snow melted by the afternoon, so I would really like for my childhood to be remedied one of these days. I love the snow, but I don't think I would if I had to endure it all the time. I enjoy watching the snow fall from inside the warmth of my home while eating mass amounts of carb-loaded food. We've been lucky this winter – it's been really mild. So far, we've only seen flurries. I heard it stays cold and snows until the end of March, so I'm not holding my breath.

Hugh recently bought me a beautiful, cream-colored Balmain coat from Bergdorf's because I have nothing "fancy" enough for Paris. Not to mention, I've never really owned a heavy coat; there was no need for one in Charleston. This coat costs more than our rent, or anything else I own. Did I just say "our" rent? I think I did. I'm *really* getting used to referring to things as *us, we,* and *our*. I'm glad I moved in with Hugh. It makes things *so* much easier. I can still hop on the elevator and go down a few floors to visit Cabot and Cooper to get some girl time in if I want. I'm just glad he asked me to move in with him. We hardly ever see each other at work, except when we go in together each morning, so it's nice to see him at *our* place.

Luckily, we didn't have to go into the office like the rest of the employees at *Hearst* since we leave for Paris this week. Cabot is still quite miffed she didn't win the contest back in December. Once she got home from the Caribbean, we went out to eat and talked a lot about what happened while she was away – the craziness that Courtney and Emma put me through and how I ended up winning the contest after all was said and done. I would still let her go in my place if I could. Then again, I wouldn't, and I'm not so sure she would do the same for me. This is a once-in-a-lifetime opportunity. I know that sounds cliché, but it's true. I wouldn't want her to give up this opportunity for me. I hope she still plans to visit once we're settled in despite her stoic outlook on the situation.

•••

I can't wait to spend the next few months in the most romantic city on this planet. Paris is going to be magical for Hugh and me, and it will help move our relationship to the next level, I hope. I'm not sure what level that is yet since we've only been dating for like five whole minutes. It just feels more serious than that. I feel like I've been with Hugh for years, but not so long that I'm already wearing underwear up to my boobs and forgetting to brush my teeth in the morning. Just long enough that I feel like I can be myself, and he can, too, without the dynamic of our relationship changing. I wouldn't mind becoming an old married couple though. There are far worse things in life than becoming *that* couple.

# Two

## Nostalgia for the Win

It's the eve of our trip to Paris, and all Hugh wants to do is act like nothing is going on in our world – as if we're just having a regular Friday night and nothing is out of the ordinary. He says it's how he keeps his anxiety down before a major event. I'm sorry, but I can't do that! I'm excited and nervous. I can't stop thinking about it! He just wants to get dinner and go to the movies as if we have nothing better to do. All I want to do is stay home, cozy by the fire, searching the streets of Paris on Google Earth for the best bakeries and places to shop. When I arrive tomorrow, I will feel like I know my way around considering I've spent a copious amount of time on this thing in the past twenty-four hours. I guess there really isn't anything to do at home – everything is packed up and placed by the door. We have no food in the fridge, except the food we're eating for breakfast, because we had to clean it out. I don't want to get anything dirty before we go. I guess I'll oblige and go on one last date in New York so Hugh can be happy.

"Have you met the guy who's subletting our place while we're gone?" I ask Hugh with slight fear in my voice.

"Actually, I have not met the guy, but I've had many chats over the phone with him. He seems like a nice fellow," Hugh says, nonchalantly, glancing up from his computer.

"Don't you think we should have met with him to make sure he's not some kind of serial killer or pedophile?!" I demand with all seriousness.

"The apartment did a thorough background check on him, love. I think we will be quite alright," Hugh says, looking at me like I'm some crazy lady.

"If you say so. Not like he'll want to steal any of *my* stuff. I, literally, packed every nice item I own for this trip. Your stuff, though, worries me," I say while pointing to his seventy-inch, television mounted over the fireplace.

"I have all that's important sitting right next to me," Hugh says as he puts his hand on my thigh.

"Could you be *any* sweeter?" I say as I pull him in for a kiss.

•••

After everything that happened over Christmas, I was fearful that Hugh and I would break up or things wouldn't be the same. I was wrong. Everything got better for us. It's like we suddenly trusted and relied on each other more than we ever had before. I don't know how I got so lucky to have Hugh as my boyfriend, but I won't ever question it or take him for granted. I'm never going to leave him in the dark again. It's honesty from here on out. Just call me Honest Abe. No more lies for me. I feel like I can finally walk around without looking over my shoulder to see if Hugh's insane ex-wife, Emma, is lurking around the corner. The good news is, she moved to California because she got a job in L.A. as a model for some company that sells vegan runway clothes. I don't care what she's doing, as long as she's very far away, which she is, thank GOD.

•••

I don't see how Hugh can focus on this stupid movie when all I can think about is sipping espresso under the Eiffel Tower and riding bicycles with baguettes in the basket. My mind is not engaged on whatever is on this very large IMAX screen. I have a hard enough time focusing on these two-hour movies when I *don't* have to leave the country.

All I can think about is my future and where I'm headed. When I was in college, I never imagined working in the fashion industry, outside of working at some boutique, or writing freelance pieces for the local galas in town. I guess I didn't dream big enough. It's hard to picture myself working for *Cosmopolitan* at Paris Fashion Week much less working at *Cosmopolitan* in New York. I wake up for work, every single day, wondering how I got so lucky to keep my job after everything that happened last fall. I constantly question how I was able to keep working at *Cosmo* despite the drama that ensued with Courtney and Emma. I know everything happens for a reason, but I'm still trying to figure out what the reason is. My instinct tells me that it's going to be taken from me one of these days. Until then, I'm going to be humble and grateful.

As I predicted, Hugh suggests we take a cab home and go to bed early. I suppose he could have thought of that before he dragged me to this movie. As we're leaving the movies, I recognize a tall, lanky, hipster-looking girl standing near the edge of the sidewalk.

"Claire!"

I'm shocked to see her on the Upper East Side at this time of night. The shock is evident in my voice. "What are you doing on this side of town?!" I ask, because she doesn't typically venture outside of her normal, ten-block radius. A stoop kid never leaves his stoop! That's Claire for you.

"Hi, Scarlett! Hi, Hugh!" Claire exclaims in a chipper tone of voice. "I'm just coming out of a movie with my girlfriend, Louise. She lives on this side of town. How have you been?" Claire asks.

I can tell Claire thinks Hugh is good-looking by the way she's clocking him up and down. You know, the way you do when you're checking someone out. I don't typically pay attention to random girls doing this to my boyfriend because it happens so often, but when your best friend's sister does it, you notice.

"We're great, Claire. Thanks for asking," I say, annoyed, because she's still staring at Hugh like he's a slice of red velvet cake.

"Hugh and I are flying to Paris in the morning for twelve weeks. *Hearst Magazines* is sending a select few from each syndicate to work Paris Fashion Week. We're super excited!"

"Wow. That sounds incredible," Claire sincerely says, to my surprise.

"How romantic to go with your boyfriend to Paris for three months. I'm jealous!"

*I'm sure you are*, I think to myself.

"I've invited Addison to come during her spring break, but I doubt she'll have time. You are both more than welcome to visit us while we're there," I say hoping she won't actually come. I like Claire, but I've never seen this side of her – she and her *hungry eyes*, that is.

"Addison and I went on a Euro trip with our parents when Addison was in middle school and I was in high school. We loved it despite being dragged to every museum. I'm sure we would appreciate it more as adults," she says, looking at Hugh with her curious eyes.

"Hugh has been to Europe several times. This is my first time leaving the country. I'm excited and nervous, but ready to be there more than anything! I will send you some pictures once I'm there."

Yea, some pictures of my boyfriend kissing me under the Eiffel Tower. The one you are currently fixated on staring at.

"Sounds like a plan. You two have fun! Great seeing you," Claire says as she awkwardly hugs my neck.

I know I shouldn't feel this way about Claire, but I'm starting to become a bit possessive over Hugh. I'm sure she didn't mean anything by it. We say our goodbyes and get in our respective cabs to go home. I guess I'm glad I was able to see a friendly face before leaving the country. It's like my mom called her to tell her to stalk me to make sure I'm okay. I hate that I'm not able to hug my real family goodbye before leaving, but that might make leaving harder.

Once Hugh and I get out of Upper Eastside traffic, I sit in the car, quietly, looking at our surroundings. I feel like the city has become my home after living here since October. I never thought living up north would be so thrilling. I look at all of the people walking in the street, pushing their babies in strollers, people talking on their phones, vendors who sell ridiculous scarves that look and feel nothing like Burberry, and realize this place has its quirks... but I *love* it. I know I'll miss New York City when I'm in Paris.

"Is Shake Shack open at 11 p.m.?" I ask Hugh, because I don't really know the answer to this question. "I don't even know why I'm hungry, but maybe I just want one last nostalgic meal before we leave the country. I could really use a burger and fries right about now."

"I think there's one location open until midnight. We should swing by the one uptown before we go home. I could go for a milkshake myself," says Hugh as he holds my hand in the backseat.

"I'm glad you don't judge me for my salty vices. I just need something delicious before we can't have it for a few months," I say, feeling a little bit like an orca.

"I take it the five-star restaurant I took you to earlier wasn't *exactly* what the doctor ordered?" Hugh asks glibly.

"It was wonderful, but the portions were *so* tiny that you're bound to be hungry in a matter of two hours after eating. When the entrée came, I thought it was another appetizer. I enjoyed it thoroughly; I just need this since we won't be able to get it tomorrow before our flight leaves."

"I'm just giving you a hard time, my love. I wouldn't have taken you there for dinner had I known," says Hugh as he pulled my hair out of my face in such an endearing way.

"You're sweet, babe. I think having this late night food run is more fun anyways!" I say with excitement in my voice because I am actually excited to go to a fast food joint with my very *sophisticated* boyfriend.

There's nothing better than Shake Shack when you're craving it. I'm pretty sure I've gained ten pounds since moving to the city and dating Hugh. He has a very refined palate; he will fit right in living in France. I hear the food in France is great, but you have to know what and how to order your dish. They prepare a lot of their dishes with heavy sauces, and that's not something I'm excited about being that I'm not too fond of condiments. All of my friends made fun of me at the lunch table in middle school because I was the kid with a plain turkey sandwich or a peanut butter and jelly. I think it's good to know what I like. Hugh isn't a picky eater, so he's always whipping up fancy meals in our apartment. I love when Hugh cooks. I love even more that we both share a passion for food and being in the kitchen.

•••

Now that our cravings have been satisfied, and we're back home, it's time to get tucked into bed and rest peacefully before our big adventure begins tomorrow. I've never had flight anxiety until now, but I'm worried about this very long trip and the jet lag everyone is so *kindly* reminding me of every chance they get. I know I'm going to be exhausted; that's a no-brainer. Hugh bought each of us some noise-canceling headphones and Tempurpedic neck pillows to help ease the annoyances of flying overseas. I doubt I'll be able to sleep, but I have a feeling Hugh and I can occupy each other in another kind of way. We still don't know our living situation once we get there, so this might be our last night beside each other for a while. I guess we better make it last...

# Three

## Oui, Oui Bebe

You know how Mrs. McAllister wakes her husband up on "Home Alone" when they almost miss their flight? That's us this morning! It's rare for me to have my stuff in a pile before he does. I couldn't sleep, so I got up and did my hair and make-up. I always seem to go to the airport looking like a homeless person, but this is PARIS! I want to start this little *jaunt* with some pride and prove I was destined for the fashion industry.

"Hugh! Wake up! We have exactly one hour to be at the airport to check in. Get out of bed!" I shout over him, trying to express my seriousness.

"I'm awake, love! You had me up *all night* if you know what I mean. I feel a bit drained from our bedtime activities."

"I'm sorry! We have to go. I have all of our stuff by the door, and I'm dressed and ready to leave right now. I called your driver, and he said he would be here in ten minutes," I say, pulling the covers off of Hugh to get him moving.

"I only need five minutes to shower and put my outfit on that you so *kindly* laid out last night," Hugh says, crawling out of bed.

As if my anxiety wasn't already through the roof, Hugh decides to sleep in on the most important day of my career with *Cosmo*. I can't be late or miss my flight due to the fact that my boyfriend needs his *beauty* rest. I love him, dearly, but I don't think he realizes how important this is to me. He knows that I like to be on time for things pertaining to work. I know Hugh is probably tired of my "type A" tendencies, but he will get used to it one of these days. I really like to come off as fearless and put together, but when things aren't going as planned, I panic.

I guess now isn't the time to tell Hugh that I'm *late*. Not late in the way he's about to make us for our flight. Late as in I haven't started my period yet... a good five days late. I tend to do this every other month – panic at anything out of the ordinary with my body. Since we started dating, Hugh has said he would love to be a father and have lots of kids, *one day*. Of course, I'm not ready. I'm not even twenty-three yet, but if I knew I could be with Hugh the rest of my life, I would be ready. The idea of having Hugh's baby, and spending my life with him, isn't scary to me. Okay, it's a little scary to think about having a baby... mostly the physical act of pushing a baby out, not the raising aspect.

I want to be comfortable on the plane, so I decide on black leggings, a soft, Free People sweater dress that my grandmother gave me, and black Ugg boots. I look cute, but not unkept, thankfully. Most of the time, when I wear Free People, I end up looking ragged. It's shocking how pricey their clothes are. I didn't want to pack my new dress coat because I'm afraid it will wrinkle, so I'm wearing that on the plane. If I'm pregnant, I won't be able to wear this coat much longer. Might as well wear it while I can. It probably looks way too fancy to be wearing with this getup, but I'm sure nobody will care, or notice. It won't matter what I'm wearing if I don't make it to the airport on time. I'm about to leave and meet Hugh there if he can't hurry up.

"I'm ready! I'm at the door. Where are you?" Hugh asks as I'm in the bathroom gathering last minute things to throw in my purse.

"Be right there!" I shout with a confidence in my voice.

"Who's the late one now, missy?" Hugh shouts back with a chortle.

"Very funny," I giggled, even though I don't think he heard my smartass tone.

When I said I wasn't going to lie to Hugh anymore, I meant it. I feel bad keeping things from him, but I plan on telling him as soon as I can take a pregnancy test.

•••

Five minutes later we're on the elevator with all of our stuff, and I finally feel like we're making moves in the right direction. Hugh's driver, Freddie, is always on time and waiting outside of the car to open the doors, or put anything in the trunk we need help with if we are traveling. Hugh recently decided to hire him, permanently, because when I moved in he realized we would be going to a lot of places together. Thank God I don't have to battle the subway station anymore or hail myself a cab. Yes, I know, I'm a bit spoiled, but I think it's really sweet Hugh wants me to be comfortable traveling around the city. Freddie has been driving for thirty years, and he says after we don't need him anymore, he'll retire. Makes Hugh and me feel like we're holding him hostage, but Freddie says it's not a problem. Maybe driving us is his way of not having to retire; it's most definitely his wife who's ready for him to come home and take it easy with her. I don't blame him – I hear once you retire you just go home to die.

Since Freddie knows we are in a major hurry to check our bags, he drove extraordinarily fast today to ensure we make it on time. Apparently, you have to check your bag two hours prior for international flights – something I wasn't aware of until last night when Hugh told me over our first dinner at *Butter*. This entire trip is going to be a huge learning curve. I feel like I learn something new everyday while dating Hugh. The other day, I was made aware that Hugh is allergic to peanuts – something I never knew until I was eating candy from my stocking and asked him if he liked Reese's Cups, my favorite chocolate. I always wondered why he didn't have peanut butter in his pantry. I wonder if our baby would be allergic to peanuts, too. I'm still trying to get over the fact I could be pregnant. You would think it bothered me more. I guess I've realized lately that crazy things happen to me, and I just have to go with it. My life is seriously something you read about in a book or see in a movie. It just doesn't seem real.

"Thank you for the ride, Freddie." I say, closing the door to his car.

"We're lucky to be alive after how fast you got us here. I'm not complaining. I wish you could come to Paris with us and drive us around, but the streets of France are wild," Hugh says as he leans over the passenger door to talk to Freddie through the window.

"I'll miss you! See you in a few months. Enjoy your time off and do something nice for yourself," I say while trying to get Hugh to move towards the door.

"Always my pleasure to drive you love birds around," Freddie says, tipping his driving cap down to signal his goodbye. "I'll miss seeing your faces and hearing about your life on the daily. Send me some pictures, will you?" he pleads.

"Of course we will, Freddie," exclaims Hugh, shaking his hand through the window on the passenger side.

•••

It seems like everyone and their brother are at LaGuardia today. Why are there so many people in New York City? I just don't get how there could be this many people traveling today. I guess I'm feeling a bit cranky from not sleeping very well last night. Not to mention my lower back is killing me. The kind of throbbing that won't stop unless you're on a piping hot heating pad while watching every episode of "Friends" and eating a gallon of ice cream.

"Excuse me, ma'am. Your bag is over the weight limit. You're going to need to remove some things in order to fly today," says Cheryl at the Delta counter with her cheap blue eye shadow and bright red lipstick.

First of all, I do not appreciate being called "ma'am", even if I'm a Southerner. Secondly, this lady, Cheryl, has no sympathy. You can look at her and tell she's tired and deals with this all day. I want to ask for a break, but I know that everyone she deals with wants a *break*. I would get tired of wearing the same skirt-suit and bandana around my neck if I did this for a living. Bless her heart.

"Can't I just pay the overage fee and be done with this, ma'am?"

"Well, you can, but it will cost $150 since you are thirty pounds over the limit," she says with no hesitations.

It's like I'm reliving moving here all over again. I do this every single time. I *really* should have hired someone to pack for me.

"Scarlett, just let me pay for this. I have an expense credit card the magazine gives me for travel. They won't know it's not for me," Hugh pleads, trying to relieve my stress and get us to our gate on time.

"If you're serious, that would be great. I don't have $150 to drop on luggage today," I say with tears drowning my eyes.

"Not a problem, my love. Please don't cry," Hugh says while touching my cheek.

Hugh is always bailing me out of crappy situations like this. I'm starting to feel bad about how much he spends on me. I know I shouldn't considering the money he makes, but I still feel dependent on him more than I should. The nice thing about it is that I get to save a lot of the money I make now that we live together. Not having to pay for rent and utilities saves me a bundle each month. I guess if there's a baby on the way we should really consider saving more money and not spending so much on frivolous things like five-star restaurants and 3D movies.

Now for my favorite part of the airport experience – security and TSA. I just love having to take my shoes off in a filthy ass airport and place all of my nice belongings in plastic, gray bins. I'm struggling to carry all of my items and dig out my passport to hand to the agent working our line. I always feel like they're judging my passport photo as if I'm supposed to look good in this picture. Nobody looks good on these things. Even Hugh has a bad photo, and I didn't think that was possible.

"Enjoy your flight, Scarlett," says the agent, holding my tickets to Paris.

"Thank you, I'll try," I say as I put my passport holder back in my carry-on bag.

Being a germ freak, I have the hardest time grasping the idea of taking my shoes off for a security scan. If I wanted to haul drugs on this plane, I'm not going to put them in my shoes. That would be a dead giveaway that I'm not intelligent and want to be caught smuggling drugs. Hugh puts our belongings in the plastic bins and I walk to the body scanner eagerly waiting for this to be over.

"Stay over here for a second. I need someone to do a thorough check," says the tall agent, motioning for me to stand in place.

"What? Why?" I ask, annoyed as hell.

"Asking questions isn't helping your case, ma'am," he says as if he's more annoyed than I am.

"I haven't done anything wrong."

It's probably the baggy sweater I'm wearing. They think I'm hiding something. Truth is, I'm just bloated at the moment.

"I know, but we are just going to do a search as soon as a female agent is available," he says like it's no big deal I'm in a hurry.

"Hugh, you are just going to have to go on without me. I could be here for a few minutes. Go to our gate and make sure we have seats," I say angrily.

"I don't have to leave. I'll wait," Hugh says, standing at the end of the TSA area.

I'm standing here, waiting to get my pat down, when I see Hugh talking to one of the female agents. I'm sure he's working his usual charm on them. Just as I suspected, he told them something to get me out of this awful and embarrassing situation. I was starting to feel like a criminal standing over here waiting to have my body excavated.

"What did you tell them to let me off the hook?" I ask Hugh as I walk as fast as I can away from that nightmare.

"It doesn't matter. What matters is that we are going to make our flight," Hugh says.

"I seriously love you. You know that, right? I'm going to hold your hand until we get to our gate. I just feel so happy to have you by my side."

"You can hold my hand anytime. I love you more," Hugh says with a sweet reassurance in his voice.

I promised my grandfather I would call him when I got to my gate. I'm nervous for what he's about to tell me. I realize when looking down at my ticket that Hugh and I aren't sitting next to each other on the plane. This morning isn't going my way at all!

"Can't we ask them to upgrade my seat to first class so I can sit with you?" I ask, pleading with Hugh.

"Of course. I'll go work on that while you call Frank."

As Hugh walks to the gate counter, I realize Hugh is like my grandfather in a lot of ways. He would do anything to take care of me and make me happy. Maybe that's why I love him so much. He reminds me of him.

•••

I dig my phone out from the abyss of my purse and call my grandfather. Thankfully, he picks up on the first ring.

"Scarlett, darling, are you alright?" Grandfather worriedly asks.

"Of course. I'm doing just fine. I'm at the gate waiting to board my flight to Paris."

"I'm excited for you, dear. I know the timing of this is just awful, but I need to tell you before you leave the country."

I'm breathing heavily, and my heart is pounding like it does when you're going into a nerve-wracking situation. I can barely speak because my mouth is completely dry… as if I need more on my plate right now.

"What? What's wrong, grandfather? Is everything alright?"

"I really hate to tell you this over the phone before you board your flight, but there is no *good* time to tell you. I know your mother wanted to tell you, but it's too hard for her right now. Your grandmother has been diagnosed with breast cancer. She's known about it for a few months and didn't tell anyone. I just found out a week ago. Otherwise, I would have told you before today. I know she'll be fine because I've secured the best doctors in the world to treat her," he says with a quiet voice as if he's ashamed.

"That is the worst news, grandfather. I really wish I hadn't known until I was there. I have a huge knot in my stomach knowing grandmother is sick and I'm leaving the country. I feel as though I need to get on a plane to Charleston to see her instead of leaving for my trip."

"No! You *must* go on your trip, baby," he says with a louder and clearer voice. "Your grandmother is a strong woman, and she will be okay. I *need* you to go on your trip and live your life. She would have told you herself, but I think she's ashamed she wasn't able to share with you sooner."

"The flight attendant is preparing us for boarding, so I need to gather my things," I say feeling guilty I'm cutting our conversation short. "I really hate that she's sick. I'm *so* sorry to hear this news. I will be in touch with you as soon as I'm settled in Paris. Please send everyone my love."

"I will, darling. I promise. Everything is going to be okay," he says before he hangs up the phone.

Wow. If that's not the icing on the cake to my rotten day, I don't know what is. How can this be happening? I just saw her at Christmas and she looked great. I guess I wouldn't have suspected her to be sick since she put on such a good act for everyone. I feel awful leaving, but I can't imagine she would want me to give up the opportunity of a lifetime to sit with her during her chemo treatments.

"What did your grandfather need to tell you?" Hugh asks with a concerned look on his face.

"First, tell me some good news. Were you able to rectify the seat situation?" I ask with low expectations.

"I hate to be the bearer of bad news, love, but the flight is full, and they can't bump someone out of first class. However, I was able to upgrade you for our return flight in April so that we will be sitting together."

"UGH!!! Are you effing serious? This day isn't going well at all. My grandmother has breast cancer! She's *very* sick. I'm leaving the country to go live out my dream, and she's at home *dying*."

"I'm so sorry to hear that. Scarlett, I know the timing of this might not be perfectly suited, but I have something to give you," Hugh says as he shuffles through his bag.

"What? What could possibly ease my mind?" I say with absolutely no hope in my voice.

I see Hugh pulling something small out of his backpack. I wasn't sure what it was, but I have a feeling it's something to make me feel better. He always has a way of making me feel better in a time of crisis.

"I know you've been anxious about this trip, rightfully so, and nervous about the flight today, too," he says while holding a small bag in his lap.

"Well, duh. I've been really anxious, and now I'm even more nervous for what you're about to give me."

"Just open it."

Hugh hands me a small wrapped gift with a red bow on top, and I eagerly tear into it like a five year old on their birthday. I don't really understand the meaning of this gift, so I ask him why he's giving it to me.

"*Good Night Moon* is supposed to ease my anxiety?" I ask with a weird look on my face.

"Well, your mom told me at Christmas that it's your favorite children's book, and it always helped calm you down in situations like this," he says with a lift in his voice hoping I'll be thankful. "I tracked down this very rare edition signed by Mary Wise Brown at *192 Books* the other day. I took you to this bookstore when we first met. Remember?" Hugh asked, hoping I would know of the small hole-in-the-wall place from four months ago, but I totally don't recall going in there.

My face turned completely pale. I felt a huge drop in my stomach. The noise around me went silent. I couldn't even look at Hugh. This book made me think of the possibility of being pregnant. How I could be reading this to *our* baby one day soon.

"This is the most thoughtful gift anyone has ever given me. I can't believe you were able to find this in the city. Thank you so much, Hugh."

"Well, you know I would do anything to make you feel better about your grandmother and this flight we're about to board. I'm really sorry you're having such a terrible day."

"I'm just upset I suck at finding clever gifts, and you are always so thoughtful," I say.

"You are the best thing that's ever been in my world. The gift is nothing. *You* are everything."

"I love you so much, Hugh Hamilton. I don't know what I'd do without you. I know that sounds trite, but it's the truth. I can't get over how sweet this gift is. I will read it on the plane," I say, hugging him as tightly as I could.

"I wish I could read it to you. I love you *more*. I'll always love you, Scarlett Hanes," Hugh says, as he looks me in the eyes to kiss me.

# Four

## First Class & No Class

I'm trying to remember the last time I had to do the yoga breathing exercises my mom taught me to calm my nerves. Oh wait, that's every single day of my life. I hate flying on planes. I seriously don't understand why I can't just go in my closet and teleport to France like "Sabrina the Teenage Witch." Why can't it be that easy? I make Hugh wait back with me at our gate, allowing everyone to board first, hoping to make this process drag out as long as possible. The thought of not being able to talk to him, or fall asleep on him, for the next six hours has me pissed, to say the least. I don't get how a flight can be *completely* full. Sometimes, I wonder if they just say that to trigger people like me on a day like today. If I see someone with some outrageous "therapy" animal, I'm going to scream bloody murder. There was a llama on someone's flight to California the other week; I saw it on the news. Who the hell brings a llama for *comfort* on a flight? Just wondering how therapeutic that can actually be. I can see a dog being comforting, but a *llama*? Whatever. Not worth harping over. Moving on.

"I don't think we can wait out here any longer," Hugh says. "We just need to rip the Band-Aid off, quickly, so it doesn't hurt as bad."

"I know, but as soon as we leave each other, it's like I'm going straight into the depths of hell," I say, rolling my eyes and growling under my breath.

"Scar, it's not that bad. I promise it will be over before you know it. Just take that sleeping medication I gave you," he says.

"Fine, but when we get to Paris will you please make this up to me?" I ask, hoping Hugh knows what I mean by that.

"I'll do my best to make it perfect," he says reassuringly.

One last kiss before we walk through the tunnel, which smells like stale air and plastic luggage. Why the flight attendants don't put air fresheners on the plane is beyond me. It wouldn't be that hard for them to use some room spray to freshen up the stench. At least there's a consistent smell you can expect at every airport and on every airplane. I guess now is the time to get on the plane. *I can do this.* I don't think I would be nervous if I was able to sit with Hugh. Something about being separated from him makes me feel like a child, lost in the mall, looking for my mom. Something about the unknown as well – flying overseas is a new experience for me. I wonder about the food they'll serve us and the people and where they're going. I'm so curious how big this plane will be and what the seats will be like – if they are comfortable or not. You know, if the plane will crash, unexpectedly, over the Atlantic Ocean. Those are the thoughts in my head right now.

"This is a HUGE plane. How does this thing stay in the air?" I ask Hugh like an ignorant fool.

"I should have warned you. It's quite large when you go on a cross-continental flight," Hugh says with a smirk because he thinks it's cute how I'm reacting.

"First class seats are SO big. I can't get over this. I'm so mad I can't sit next to you and I'm stuck in the back. I'm in row twenty-eight or something very far from you," I say, motioning to the back of the plane.

"That's not that far, actually. I think you're right behind first class if I'm not mistaken," Hugh reassuringly says.

It seems like a world away. I feel like the black sheep of this plane not being able to sit with my boyfriend in first class. Oh well, I guess I better get settled.

•••

"Hugh! I didn't know we would be on the same flight! It's great to see a familiar face," says the high-pitched voice from two aisles over.

"Hello, Jessica. Good to see you. I guess we will both be sitting in the same area for the flight. I'll come talk to you later." Hugh politely says as if it was no big thing. "Have you met Scarlett Hanes? She works for *Cosmo*," he says like I'm just some *acquaintance.*

Scarlett Hanes? Are you kidding me? How about SCARLETT is my GIRLFRIEND that I live with in my fancy apartment. Oh, boy. I'm fuming now.

"Hi, Jessica. *So nice to meet you,*" I say, even though it's the opposite of *nice.* "Whom do you work for at *Hearst?*" Like I even care.

I try to play it cool and not let her see just how jealous I was that she's about to sit three feet away from Hugh for the next six hours.

"I'm a photographer for *Harper's Bazaar* with Hugh. We've been working together for the past couple of years. He's *so* talented, as you probably already know," Jessica says all haughty and annoyingly with her big breasts out for the plane to see.

"He's my boyfriend! So, *yes,* I *do* know!" I say, shoving that bit of information in her face.

"Oh, well, how about that! I didn't know you were seeing someone," Jessica says as if she thought Hugh was still a free agent. "I knew I should've snagged you years ago. Good for you, Scarlett," Jessica confirms all *smug,* as if she just heard that her cat died.

Hugh is more than just "seeing" someone; we are LIVING together, and I might be carrying his child for gosh sakes! I'll just have to prove to Jessica how *serious* we are. If I linger, I'll look desperate, so I kiss him square on the lips, with a little tongue of course, and make my way to my seat.

"I love you, honey. I hope you have an enjoyable flight. Let me know if you need anything at all. I'll be right up here if you want to see me. Unfortunately, they won't let you come talk to me, but I'll come check on you," Hugh says in quiet voice so nobody can hear him.

"I love you, too. I hate this. More than you could fathom," I say.

"I know you do. Just think about Paris. We will be there in the morning," he says.

"Where are you running off to, Scarlett?" Jessica asks as if she doesn't already know what's about to happen. This bitch, I swear.

"They made a mistake with my ticket and put me in economy. Oh well!"

"That's too bad," she says, looking at her very large, first-class seat. "I guess we won't tell you about the food and wine we will be consuming up here! Ha-ha."

I'm going to *kill* her.

"I'll be just fine, thanks," I say with zero politeness.

I leave Hugh and make my way through the crowd of people who are taking their sweet time getting settled in their seats. I finally find myself nearing my row. I love how spacious the plane is; you don't feel as crammed as you would on a normal flight. There's a lot more head space, three aisles widely spaced, and all of them have three seats in each row. It's not like that in first class; you sit beside one person or you're in the middle to yourself. It's more private and comfortable up there. I look around at all the people on this flight thinking to myself how I got to this point. I graduated from College of Charleston. I applied to thousands of jobs. Addison submitted a fake resume, and I got the job at *Cosmo*. Sounds about right. A lot has happened leading up to this point. I know I shouldn't be complaining about my seating arrangement when I'm lucky to be on this flight at all. This is the trip of a lifetime, and I'm excited to find out what's to come.

"Hi, I think this is my seat next to you," I say in a quiet voice, hoping I don't wake the man sitting in the window seat.

"Hi, do you need help with your bags?" asks the kind, little Indian woman who has the middle seat. Thank God I don't have to be stuck in the middle for the next however long it takes to get to Europe. I can't imagine how she would be able to help me with my bag being that she's smaller than I am, but maybe she has more experience with this kind of thing than I do.

"Yes, that would be great. Thanks," I say with a reluctant tone.

I know it sucks I'm so far from Hugh, but it could be worse. I'm not sitting next to a baby, so there's that.

"Would you like me to take your coat?" she asks so kindly.

"No thanks. I'm quite cold."

"It is a bit chilly. They always have these flights extra cold so people won't get sick," she says as she takes her seat.

"I guess it's better than it being hot," I say as I squeeze into my seat. Definitely not as big as the first class seats.

"Well, is this your first time to France?" she asks, wanting to strike up conversation.

"Yes, it's my first time flying internationally, too," I reply.

"That's very exciting. I hope it's enjoyable for you," says the kind woman whose name I don't know yet.

"I hope so, too, thanks. My name is Scarlett, and you are?" I ask so that I don't have to sit next to a stranger the entire flight.

"Oh, I'm sorry. My name is Narinder. Nice to meet you, Scarlett," she says.

Narinder spent the next fifteen minutes or so telling me about her life and her family. She has a wedding dress shop in Queens and has seven kids. I love hearing about her big family and traditions they have even though I barely know this woman. She's very kind and soft spoken, but you can tell she's an intelligent, savvy businesswoman. She's owned her dress shop for over forty years and plans to leave it to her only daughter when she's old enough to take over. I tell her all about my crazy life and how I ended up living in New York City with the Quinlan's and how I work for *Cosmopolitan*. Her "oohh's" and "aahh's" were abundant when I told her how I won the contest for Paris. She seemed shocked to hear all that I've been through the past few months. I can tell this is going to be an interesting flight.

Now that we're in the air, and can't really talk to each other anymore, I decide to get settled and try to rest. I have my noise-canceling headphones on and my neck pillow Hugh got for me, and I'm trying to close my eyes and not think about how much I miss him right now. Not to mention, I can't stop worrying about my family back home. I hope I can rest knowing how sick my grandmother is. I just hope she'll be okay.

The man in the window seat is knocked out and has his mouth wide open as if he's about to catch flies. How does one fall into such a deep sleep so quickly? I guess I'd rather him be sleeping than bothering me. I want to fall asleep so I don't have to wonder what Hugh and Jessica are talking and laughing about up in first class. I'm so irritated she had to comment on Hugh's relationship status right in front of me as if I was unimportant or not standing there at all. She looked to be about Hugh's age if I had to guess. The bags under her eyes looked darker than my black leggings, so she's not in her twenties. Hopefully, she won't be chatting with my boyfriend for the next six hours and she'll choose to get some much-needed rest. She looks like she could use some. Time to take this sleeping pill and knock out. Hopefully, when I wake up, we will be close to Europe.

# Five

## Scarlett Red

"Excuse me, miss. Your dinner is here," says the flight attendant, gently tapping my shoulder to wake me.

"Oh my gosh. How long have I been asleep?" I ask Narinder.

"We've been in the air for nearly three hours, I believe," Narinder says with a coy smile on her face.

"Well then. I guess my boyfriend hasn't checked on me yet. He's in first class enjoying the finer things in life," I say to the flight attendant, as if she cares.

"Enjoy," says the flight attendant, patiently waiting on me to finish waking up while handing me the meal.

I'm looking at Narinder's meal wondering how she got something different than I did. She explained she has dietary restrictions with her religion, so they give her something to meet her requirement. I wish I had known I could have got something else. My chicken is like rubber, the dinner roll is ice cold, and the dessert is some nasty-looking pudding, if I had to guess. I can only imagine how much better Hugh's meal is up there in the swanky area of the plane. I'm really surprised he has yet to check on me. I guess I should just eat my meal and stop whining. They'll be around to scoop it up before I even get to sink my teeth into this ice roll. I don't get how you can pay so much to fly and get stuck eating this inedible crap they serve. This "food" is worse than the meal I had at the hospital when I had my tonsils taken out at ten years old. Granted, I couldn't really eat my food after the procedure because I felt as though I was swallowing shards of glass, but it looked similar to this. I decide to shovel my meal down as fast as I could so I could get up, walk around, and use the restroom. My legs feel frozen in this position and I can't move.

"Are you going to eat that?" asks Narinder, motioning to my pudding or whatever it is.

"No, you can have it… I guess," I murmur, wondering why anyone would want this damn food.

"I need to get up to use the restroom. Be right back."

"Scarlett, your coat! Oh my," exclaimed Narinder with shrill shock in her voice.

"What? What's wrong with it?" I say, turning around, trying to see my butt without people noticing.

"I think you may have started your period," she said with a quiet whisper, trying not to alert the entire row of people now staring curiously.

"Are you kidding me?! This cannot be happening. This is a *designer* coat. Not to mention, I thought I was pregnant up until now. UGH. This. Day. Sucks."

"I'm so sorry, dear. I can ask the flight attendant for some club soda."

"I don't think you're supposed to put club soda on Balmain, but thanks anyways. It's ruined."

"It won't be more ruined than it already is. Let's give it a try," Narinder says in a gentle and calming way.

I can tell she's trying to help, but she has no idea how badly I just want to sit on the floor of this plane and ball my eyes out like a toddler. I can't get over the fact that I ruined the most beautiful coat I've ever owned and I started my period. I need to talk to Hugh immediately. I don't care if I'm not supposed to go into first class. I'm doing it.

"Ma'am, you can't go up there. We have the curtains up," says the flight attendant who is clearly trying to get punched in the face.

"It's a personal emergency. Nothing too crazy, but I need to speak with my boyfriend, Hugh." I say politely, trying to have my way.

"Mr. Hamilton?" she asks.

"Yes."

There's another Hugh in first class? I think to myself with a sarcastic tone of voice.

"Ok, no problem. Just make it quick," she says, looking the other way, as if she's doing me some *grandiose* favor letting me into first class.

I push through the gray mesh curtains to find myself standing next to Hugh; he looks so peaceful and comfortable in his reclining seat. I don't want to wake him, but I'm in need of some consoling right now.

"Hugh, wake up, please!" I nudge his arm trying to wake him. I try to whisper because it appears everyone in first class is in a deep slumber.

"Scarlett?" Hugh says while clearing his throat as he wakes up from his restful sleep.

"I need to talk to you," I say with heavy discernment in my voice.

"What is it, babe?" Hugh says as he pushes his arms up to a sitting position.

"I started my period while I was wearing my coat. I'm afraid it's ruined. I'm having such a bad day. I really just want it to end."

"Oh, no. I'm so sorry, Scar! Is there anything I can do?" he worriedly asks.

"You can trade seats with me," I say sarcastically, but not really joking at all.

"I can. And I will. Just let me alert the flight attendant. I don't know why

I didn't think of that before. I'm very sorry that I didn't. I feel so inconsiderate now."

"Seriously? You would do that for me?" I ask with hope in my voice.

"Absolutely. I'll hand them your coat to see if they can rectify this situation. I'm sure we can fix it. If not, I'll buy you a new one. Maybe not Balmain, but I'll replace it so you can have a nice coat to wear," Hugh says reassuringly.

"Thank you, Hugh. I don't know what I'd do without you. I hope you don't mind sitting back in my seat. Narinder has been really kind to me. Let her know the situation. I'm sure she'll understand."

"Of course, love."

"Hugh, I have something to tell you, and I hope it doesn't freak you out."

"I'm sure I can handle it. I'm a big boy."

"I thought I was *pregnant.* I've been waiting on my period for the past five days. Had I not started by tomorrow, I was going to take a test."

"Why in the world would that freak me out? I would love if you were having our baby, but I'm relieved you aren't because this is not the perfect time for us. We need to enjoy Europe. We have a few more milestones to reach before having a baby. We will. One day."

"Well, I'm glad you have that outlook. I would definitely appreciate being engaged or married before I get pregnant," I say seriously.

"I agree. That will come, too," Hugh says.

"Thanks for being so sweet as usual. I don't know what I'd do without your never-ending love and patience."

"Just enjoy your time up here. The flight attendants will take good care of you. If you're thirsty or hungry, just let them know," Hugh says, getting up from his seat to let me take his place.

"I can't wait to eat something decent," I excitedly say.

"I love you," Hugh says as he kisses my forehead goodbye.

What I really can't wait for is the look on Jessica's face when she sees me up here instead of Hugh. I can't wait to tell her that Hugh wanted to trade seats with me so I could be more comfortable. I have a feeling it won't sit well with her. I don't care. I'm happy I have the opportunity to spend the next few hours in comfort. I know one thing – now that I'm not pregnant I am going to enjoy the biggest glass of merlot they will give me. Hopefully, they can get me something to eat that actually resembles food.

I sit my neck pillow and headphones on my seat and make my way to the lavatory. Thankfully, there isn't a line like the one in my section of the plane. Gosh, I don't know how I'll ever go back to coach after sitting in first class. I know I've sat in first class before, but an international flight is so much different. After making my toilet paper fortress, and washing my hands with this citrus-scented soap, I return to my seat to see Jess giving me the stare of death. I decide just to smile and not say anything. I'm sure she'll have something to say when we land. For now, I'm just going to sit back and relax, watch a movie, and hopefully have something to eat.

"Hello, miss. Can I get you anything?" asks the flight attendant in first class.

"What do you have?" I curiously ask.

"We have cocktails, wine, snacks, a moist towelette soaked in lavender essential oils, and the list goes on," she replies.

"I would love a *large* glass of merlot, some trail mix, and one of those cold towels, please."

"Absolutely. I'll have that out in a few minutes, Mrs. Hamilton."

What? I guess Hugh had to tell them I was his wife in order to switch seats. That name sure does have a *ring* to it. Pun intended. I feel like I just asked a genie to grant my wishes and she waved her wand and made it come true. I could get used to this.

For the rest of the flight, I managed to drink three large glasses of wine and eat all the snacks I could while watching a romantic comedy.

•••

"Good morning. We are about to serve the breakfast. What would you like, Mrs. Hamilton?"

"I would love oatmeal, an English muffin, bacon, and strawberries, please."

"And to drink?"

"I'll take a mimosa. Thank you." Now that I can drink since I'm not pregnant...

After I finished my delicious breakfast, I started to feel guilty that Hugh was sitting in my seat in the peasant section of the plane. I guess he's done this enough to allow me a chance to enjoy it. I know that he would want me to be happy. Hugh is selfless in that way. I can only hope to be more like him when I *grow up*. I click on the screen to find the map, which shows where we are located at the moment, and it appears we are fairly close to Paris. I'm getting anxious to get off of this plane. I'm excited to start the first day of the rest of my life. I know this trip is going to change everything for me.

# Six

## Smoke & Mirrors

I wake up to the sound of the captain announcing that we have arrived at Charles de Gaulle International Airport. I don't know how I slept through the landing, but I guess you wouldn't feel something like that after the sleeping pill and mimosa I had at breakfast. Perhaps the landing was very smooth and the captain of the plane did a great job. Maybe you don't feel the landing in first class with the extra padded seats.

I stand up to stretch my arms over my head and look for Hugh through the curtains. I don't want to rush back there and get stuck in the sea of jetlagged people, so I just patiently wait here for him until then. I look over to see that Jessica is applying some concealer under her eyes. She really needs it considering how tired she looks. I feel as though I should strike up a conversation with her to make her uncomfortable, but I don't really feel like doing so. Usually, I would be the bigger person, but I really don't care to be with people like her.

I bend over to pull up the window screen to see the gray skies of Paris and all the men and women running around trying to deliver luggage to the different gates. It still feels like America to me. I guess once I'm inside the actual airport it will feel very far from home. I really want to message my family to let them know I've arrived safely. I don't have cell service, so I'm just going to craft a short email to send once I get Internet connection in the airport.

"Good Morning, beautiful! I hope the rest of your flight was much smoother after taking my place," Hugh says after kissing me straight on the lips.

"Hi, babe! I'm so glad to be with you. Please don't ever leave me ever again," I say.

"It's me and you from here on out. I promise," he says while grabbing my carry-on bags.

I can't say I hate that he spoils me so much because I don't. It's wonderful to walk around and stretch my legs for the first time in hours, not to mention the fresh air after being on the same airplane for so long. My senses are overloaded right now – sight, smell, sound.

I can't get over how different it looks in here. I feel like I've gone back in time, like I'm in some kind of time warp where everything is old and outdated. The first thing I see is a small cafe in the middle of the terminal where people are sipping out of tiny espresso mugs and eating pastries. I didn't expect to see that so soon, but I guess everyone was serious when they told me that pastries are everywhere in France. I see people rushing around, carrying their luggage, and pushing their children in strollers frantically trying to make their connecting flights. That's something you see in every country no matter where you are. I hear people spouting off French words in every area of the airport. I can't understand a word of what they are saying. I feel like I might as well be deaf right now because I feel so lost and confused. I think I have a newfound sympathy for foreigners in America.

I'm glad Hugh has won this contest trip before because I have no idea what I'm doing nor do I know where I'm going. All I know is that he has requested a car to take us into Paris to where we will be living. I know it's unlikely we will be living together here, but I just hope they pair me with someone I will like. I really do wish Cabot had the opportunity to be here right now. I have a feeling she'll make her way to Paris. I hope Addison will, too, even though I know it's unlikely with her school schedule. My biggest fear is that everyone back home will forget me and will have moved on and made new friends. I guess I can't think like that or I will be sad during my stay here. I know that I'm just tired, and I'm emotional because of it. I think once we get settled, and I see the Eiffel Tower for the first time, I'll snap out of it.

We make our way through the airport to the crowded baggage claim area and wait until our bags arrive. Hugh told me that he bought the international package for his phone so I can use it whenever I need to call or message anyone. I tell him I'd like to send my email, and I don't want to get on the phone right now because it would wake them up and I don't really want to cry right now. I know that if I talk to my parents, I'll get upset because I'm still very much a train wreck about the news of grandmother.

*Dear lovely family of mine,*

*I made it to Paris, safe and sound. I can't say that I loved the flight because it felt like it took light years, but I'm excited to be here, finally. I'm not tired yet, but I know I will be soon. I will call you and try to keep you updated as often as possible. I will be sending pictures whenever I see something photo-worthy. Hope everyone is great, especially grand-mother.*

*Love you always,*
*Scarlett*

I have to keep it fresh and light or they will be upset I'm not having a good time on my trip. I know my grandfather meant well by telling me before I left, but I would have much rather found out a week into being here. I just feel like I can't enjoy myself as much knowing everyone at home is worried sick, and I'm over here drinking Rosé and eating crepes. I just need to get a hold of Savannah because I know she'll keep it real with me and let me know how everyone is *really* doing. I don't need them to sugarcoat what's going on. I need them to be real with me so I know the condition of grandmother's health. I don't want her to pass while I'm over here and not be able to share a proper goodbye. I would be devastated if that happened.

"Scarlett, are you alright, love?" Hugh worriedly asks.

"Sorry. I'm just zoning out. I'm very tired, and I feel bad about leaving knowing how sick my grandmother is."

"You have to know that Lucy would want you here. She'll be okay. I know everyone is taking great care of her. You have to be happy. You're in the city of love with *your* love. Please be happy. It will be okay. I see our bags – I'm going to grab them and then we will be on our way," Hugh says as he jogs towards the conveyer belt to pick up our luggage.

"Okay. I'll be here with our stuff. Thanks."

I just want to get out of these clothes that I bled through and take a shower. I want to lie on a bed and be comfortable for the first time in days. I want to unpack and get settled. It doesn't even feel real to be standing at this airport. I don't think it hit me that I'm in another country. I'm in France. Hell, I'm in Europe. I guess I didn't even realize we're six hours ahead of Eastern Time, either. I mean, I knew we would be in a different time zone, sure; I just didn't put much thought into it. It's seven thirty-five in the morning here, so I guess it's one thirty-five in the morning at home. I've stayed out later than that, so I'm not that tired, honestly. I think when five in the morning, U.S. time rolls around-the jet lag will hit me. Everyone has told me to fight the jetlag and stay awake, but I don't think I'll have that kind of willpower.

We're supposed to meet up at a hotel in the middle of the city with everyone that will be working for *Hearst* during the next few months. I think we will all be staying in this hotel for the first few days until we can figure out living arrangements. You better believe I'll be staying with Hugh if I have my way. I'm not in the mood to deal with foolishness today. If they stick me in a room with a stranger and expect me to sleep in the same room with her right off the bat, they're high. I think that's why they give us rooms in the hotel for a few days, so we can meet everyone and see how we mesh together. Let's just hope they put me with someone I can get along with who doesn't mind me having my boyfriend over all the time. I guess I wouldn't appreciate it if they had their boyfriend over all the time, but who doesn't like Hugh? I will figure out a solution. Maybe I can tell them I need to live alone so I can focus on doing the best possible job or I can tell them I have a really loud snoring condition, which keeps people up if they have to sleep in the same room with me. I don't want to be "that" girl, but I will if I have to.

Hugh motions to the car outside while dragging our luggage on a cart. "It's time to go now, love. Our car is waiting."

"Okay, I'm ready."

I see Jessica struggling to carry all of her luggage, and I feel kind of bad she is headed for the REN station when we're getting in a Mercedes. I guess I could be polite and let her ride with us, but she probably already purchased her train ticket and wouldn't want to ride in the car with me. I'm sure if I weren't here, she'd ask to ride with Hugh. Sadly, I wonder if I wasn't here if *he* would ask *her* to ride with him. There are a lot of things I wonder about if I weren't here. Would Hugh still love me or want to remain in a relationship? Would he cheat on me? Would he be so busy with everyone from work that he wouldn't have time to talk to me? I guess I can't think like that since we are lucky enough to be together. Gosh, I don't know why my mind is wandering so much today. I will just blame it on my period and the emotional rollercoaster my hormones have me on. I would certainly like to get off this rollercoaster as soon as possible and return to my normal self.

•••

Once we're outside, and I breathe in fresh air, I notice that it's not the same fresh air we have back home. The air smells smoky and polluted. I didn't think it was possible to smell worse than New York, but Paris has succeeded to do so. There's a haze in the air from all the smog and cigarette smoke. Everyone around us is smoking cigarettes, even teenagers, sadly. I hate to see a young kid destroying their health like that. In fact, I hate that anyone would destroy their health with cigarettes.

The cars are so tiny here, and everyone is driving like maniacs out of the terminals. I thought things were wild in NYC, but I was wrong. This is a whole new ball game here in France. I'm nervous to even get in this car, but I'm hoping it's an easy and pleasurable experience. I feel like I've entered the twilight zone and I have no idea where I am. I feel like nothing is familiar. I want to see something that feels familiar; a remnant of home. I'm scared, for the first time in a long time, about where I'm headed and what will happen. I thought I would feel excited and happy to be here, but I feel the exact opposite. Hugh seems to be keeping his cool, but he's been here before to know what to expect. I think the fear of the unknown has me completely unraveled. I'm sure I'll feel better as soon as I can get some food and take a nap.

# Seven

## Is This Real Life?

The driver sat in the car and didn't get out to help us with our belongings or open our door as Freddie would so kindly do at home. I wish he were here to help us. Hugh and I managed to stuff everything in the small trunk of this black Mercedes. I don't know if it's just my imagination, but I feel like this car is smaller than the ones at home. I guess I will have to adjust to all of these nuances and get over it. People don't like change, and I fall into that category of people. I like change when it comes to my wardrobe and the new season of the "Bachelorette," but this is way too much change.

"Bonjour, Madame and Monsieur," says the French driver.

"Bonjour," Hugh and I chime at the same time.

It feels so funny to say that. I think this is the first time I've said it out loud besides when I was practicing at home.

"Where will we be going today?" asks the driver in broken English.

"We're going to the Peninsula on Avenue Kleber," Hugh says to the driver.

"Where is the Peninsula, babe?" I curiously ask.

"It's a beautiful, five-star hotel in the middle of the city where events for Paris Fashion Week take place. It's luxurious, and you will love it. I've stayed there once for this contest."

"How long will we get to stay there?" I ask as I look out the window, hoping to see something interesting.

"I'm not sure how they are doing it this year. I just know that's where we will be meeting and most likely staying for the weekend. I have a surprise for you, but I can't tell you until we're there."

"A good surprise I hope. I've had a rough day. I would love something good to happen," I say looking down at my hands in my lap.

"I think you'll be pleasantly surprised," Hugh says with a half smirk like he's up to no good.

I'm sure Hugh knew before we got here that I would have my claws out and be on edge, so he took things into his own hands in order for his girl to be happy. I can't say I blame him. If I had known I would be this upset, I would have done something nice for myself, too. I can only imagine what this surprise might be.

For the duration of the lengthy ride into the city, I look out the window noticing all the extravagant architecture, scaffolding, and details. I'm amazed at how beautiful a city can be considering how old it is. You can tell the sun is trying to come out from the clouds, and the morning is turning into the afternoon. I'm so glad things are starting to turn around. All of a sudden I feel emaciated, but I do feel happier which usually doesn't happen when I'm hungry. I'm hoping when we get to the hotel they will serve us lunch or have some kind of reception.

"Look! It's the Eiffel Tower! Holy shit!" I shout with excitement.

"Isn't it amazing?" Hugh asks as he puts his arm around me.

"YES. Oh my God! I can't believe I'm here. I can't believe I'm seeing this. Let me roll the window down so I can take a picture," I say, grabbing my phone to snap a shot of this masterpiece.

"Scarlett, just take it all in. We will be living here for the next three months. You will have so many opportunities to take pictures in front of this marvel," Hugh says.

"I just want to take one to send to my family. Just let me soak it all in now so I can be happy," I demand.

"Alright, alright. Go ahead. Do your thing," Hugh laughs.

I can't believe my eyes. I'm staring directly at the Eiffel Tower. I can't seem to take my eyes off of it. It's the most incredible thing I've ever seen. I didn't expect to feel this way about a landmark, but I have never seen something so extraordinary; something so magnificent. I can't believe this is my life. This is *real* life. How did I get so lucky? I don't get how I deserve such luck. There are so many people that will never have the opportunity to fly to Paris and see the Eiffel Tower. I get to see it for the next twelve weeks. I'm living out every girl's dream. I'm living a real life fairytale. Sometimes I wonder what I did in this life to get so lucky. I constantly wonder how my life came to this very moment. It's as if I am living inside of some imaginary alternate universe – that universe being with my perfect boyfriend, Hugh, and this beautiful city I'm already falling head over heels for. I'm so glad my outlook and mood has shifted.

"Why didn't you tell me this place was so beautiful?" I ask.

"I wanted to see the look you have on your face right now. It's priceless," says Hugh as he smiles all coy like he planned this in his head.

"Oh, is that right?" I ask sarcastically.

"Yes. It's adorable. You're adorable," he says.

"Well, I'm glad you didn't tell me. I'm happy to provide you with this amusement," I jokingly say.

"It's perfectly alright to be smitten with this city," Hugh says like he's about to tell a story. "The first time I came here, I had the same look on my face that you have had since we left the airport. It's Disney Land for adults. Just wait until you try the wine at the bistro with the perfect view of the Eiffel Tower at sunset. I plan on taking you there many times while we're here."

"I can't wait for that. There're so many things I want to do with you here. You being one of those things," I say while squeezing Hugh's thigh in the back of this cab.

"Is that a fact?" I ask. "I couldn't agree more."

You could cut the sexual tension in this car with a knife. Hugh and I are going to need to live near each other or this is going to drive us mad. I know the living situation can't be ideal for us, but we will learn to miss each other. It's going to be hard going from the penthouse to the outhouse – not to mention living with females. The idea of living with girls again makes me want to pull out my hair. When you get used to living with the opposite sex, you realize how crazy females are. Hugh has taught me how to be more realistic with my life and expectations – how to be content and still with my life; I feel like women are never content and they always want more. We're our own kind of breed, that's for sure. I know I'm guilty of those things.

"We're here. This is us," Hugh says to the driver as he tries to tell him in French. It's so sexy hearing my Australian boyfriend try to speak a foreign language with his already appealing accent.

"Is this the hotel we're staying at this weekend?" I ask, looking up at this marvelous hotel.

"Yes, this is the Peninsula, one of the most luxurious hotels in all of Paris. You're going to love it." Hugh says, smiling from ear to ear, knowing he's made me very happy.

"Is this *real* life?" I can't stop asking that question.

"I'm afraid it is. I hope you're happy," Hugh says.

"Happy? Are you kidding me? I don't think happy is a good enough word to describe my ebullience," I say while snapping photos on my phone. "I can't wait to send these to my sister."

"Well, good. I think you'll love it. I suggested it to the events board mainly because I knew my girlfriend would enjoy it," says Hugh.

"You're on some events board now?" I ask with my eyebrows raised.

"I just make suggestions and they listen to me. Mostly women on that board if you catch my drift; hate to say I have a way with the ladies," boasts Hugh.

"You don't have to tell me. I already know how you swoon your way through life. I know you are capable of getting away with murder. Trust me," I say with my arms crossed and one leg out, proving my point.

"As long as you are aware and okay with it," Hugh says with a giggle.

I've never heard Hugh brag before now, but I guess when in Rome. Or… when in Paris. Good for him, though. To have a way with people is a gift. If only I could work that kind of magic on people. Maybe if we ever move to Australia, I'll lose my southern accent and have a way with people like he does. Not likely, but a girl can dream.

•••

Everything in this hotel lobby looks expensive; everything and *everyone* for that matter. From their head to their toes, they are decorated in the finer things in life. Not to mention, they're all pretty people. They say that Charleston has some beautiful women. Well, Paris has you beat, Chuck Town. Women with long, shiny hair and mile-high legs to compliment their long hair, and everyone is thin and fit looking. I have a feeling I'm amongst supermodels. I don't see anyone I recognize from work yet, but I'm guessing they will be trickling in at various times. I don't think I've ever stepped foot in a nicer hotel than this. The bar is set very high for me now. This is what I like to call the "cream de la cream" of hotels. All of the walls are marble and have tall ceilings. The floor is black and white checker tile, and the counters are black marble. The hotel is decorated with modern furnishings, and you can tell a lot of money was spent on the décor. When I was looking up hotels in college, I could only see hotels like the Mercure because it's all I could afford. I thought I was going to study abroad here, but it didn't work out for me, unfortunately. It wasn't because of money or anything; I didn't have enough credits to take a semester off, so I had to stay back to take health class of all things. What a joke.

As Hugh checks us in, I wait in the lobby area and try to get Internet connection so I can message my family. I just want to let them know I'm alive and well, and that I'm in the nicest building I've ever stepped foot in my whole life. My mom thinks nothing of this kind of thing; she grew up super privileged, traveling the world, visiting the finer places for most of her life. She's been all over Europe with my dad when they were younger. After they got married, they spent three weeks hopping from one country to the next, being wined and dined by Roger. That was probably where I was conceived if I had to guess. I finally connect to the Wi-Fi and email my family the message I crafted earlier. It wouldn't send at the airport, so they might be worried sick about me... or they don't care and they think I'm doing just fine. Who knows? All I know is that I'm already missing them. I'm going to think of my grandmother every single day until I come home.

# Eight

## Bougielicious

Whoever decided we should stay at the Peninsula for an entire weekend in Paris is my new best friend. This bougie-ass hotel has me on cloud nine. I could see how celebrities want to live in hotels, or stay at them for weeks on end. I could find myself locked in one of these rooms for days without leaving. I don't know how Hugh managed to get us a room together, but I guess he worked some of that charm we know so well. As my grandfather would say, "I ain't mad atcha," and he said it a lot. I feel you on that, grandfather. I'm incredibly happy with this room situation. Not to mention, they upgraded us to the garden suite, and let me tell you something, that doesn't sound very fancy, but it is at this hotel. I'm not sure why they upgraded us unless Hugh is paying for it, but I doubt he would drop four thousand euros a night. Yes, you heard me right – that is the price of luxury.

"Babe, come look in here. We have a dining room table we can eat breakfast at in the morning," I shout to Hugh from the other room.

"That's what you're excited about? A dining room table?" he asks with shock in his voice.

"Well, I've never been in a hotel room this big before," I say.

"Why don't you come on this terrace we have? The views are incredible. I wouldn't mind staying in here with you the entire time. Getting intimate and what not," Hugh shouts from the bedroom.

The idea of staying in this luxurious hotel room all weekend with Hugh sounds amazing. I don't even care about sightseeing. It would be nice to utilize this room since we will be able to see Paris for the next three months. I wouldn't mind staying here, ordering some champagne and room service, eating dinner on our lovely terrace, and making love to Hugh all night.

"You read my mind. I think we should stay in all weekend. Just be together. We need to rest from all the traveling and time difference anyways, don't you think?" I ask hoping he'll agree.

"Couldn't agree more, love," Hugh says.

This bathroom looks like something I've seen on a "Batman" movie, or maybe "James Bond." You walk in and see a closet on each side, with hangers for your clothes, and a dressing area lit for a movie star. I'm waiting for this wall to turn into some hidden room with a jewelry vault or something crazy. Everything looks brand new as if they decorated prior to our arrival. I mean, seriously, what hotel room has a towel drying rack? Apparently, that's common in France since they don't really use dryers for their clothes and linens. Shiny black marble countertops with a huge Jacuzzi bathtub and an extra large walk-in shower with glass doors. Every inch of wall space is covered in white and gray marble. I have a thing for white and gray marble for whatever reason; I just love the style. I love how they give you these expensive toiletries at hotels like this. I've never had such amazing smelling body wash and shampoo in my life.

"Hugh, come in here and take a shower with me before we have to go do work things," I say.      "Don't you want to get dirty first?" he asks.

"I'm already dirty from traveling. Just get in here with me!" I demand.

"I like it when you're bossy with me. It turns me on," he says.

I undress from head to toe and enter the large, glass, walk-in shower and pull Hugh into my body to kiss him all over. The showerhead is like a waterfall, pouring onto us, with the additional showerhead beating down on our bodies. *Double* penetration if you will. I washed our bodies with the soap and continued to make out with Hugh, and he puts his hands further down my body to please me like I've never felt before. This is a scintillating feeling he's giving me. Something about this expensive soap is probably creating the perfect amount of friction. I could stay in here all night long and let him do this to me.

Just as things were heating up, I realized I'm on my period. Gosh. I knew this day was too good to be true. I *would* be staying at this amazing hotel and not be able to have sex all weekend. Its like Courtney knew, and she's punishing me from afar. Very unlikely, obviously, but it would be like her to know my cycle and plan everything around it. Courtney emailed me the other day making sure I knew I had to work hard while I was in Paris, as if I didn't know that. She has me under the microscope now that she knows the truth about me. I guess I had to expect that. It's better than being fired. I think she'll eventually trust me again, but I don't know when that will be. I'm sure after being away from her for three months she'll realize all that I do for *Cosmo*. Maybe some distance will be good for us. I'll prove to her I am trustworthy through all my hard work while I'm here.

•••

The afternoon nearly slipped by when we both realized it's seven at night and we are supposed to be at some meet and greet at eight. We went into a deep slumber after our incredible shower together. I feel like a zombie, like I could sleep for days. I thought we would be able to stay in all night and feed each other chocolates and drink wine, but I forgot they slipped an itinerary under our door when we got here. I'm hoping this little shindig doesn't last too long. The last thing I want to do is put makeup and real clothes on. I wonder if it would be acceptable to wear sweatpants to meet everyone? I doubt it. I honestly don't care what they think of me because they will form their opinions whether I'm dressed to the nines or look like I just rolled out of bed. That's just how people are, unfortunately.

"What are you wearing to this thing, babe?" I ask, shuffling through my suitcase.

"I'm just going to wear jeans, a white shirt, and a black blazer," Hugh says as he neatly pulls his garments out of his bag.

"I'm stressing out because I can't find anything to wear. After seeing the women in the lobby today, I feel like a peasant."

"You're not a peasant, I promise. You're exactly who I want you to be. You're lovely."

"Well, I feel dumpy. I guess you'll have to show me where all the great shopping is in the city."

"Of course. I know plenty of places to take you."

"Awesome. I can't wait."

I decided to wear a simple outfit of black jeans and a cute blouse I got at Luna's when I went home for Christmas. I don't want to dress up too much because I have no idea what we're going to be doing at this thing. All I know is there better be some kind of dinner there because I totally skipped lunch today. It's definitely lunchtime in America, so I'm ready to chow down. I'm nervous about what the food will be like and what I'll have to endure for the next few months. I guess the worst-case scenario is eating at McDonald's for the duration of my trip. My fear is showing up and not knowing what the hell is on the platter they're serving. I feel ignorant in so many ways since I'm not a seasoned traveler. I blame my parents for not bringing me anywhere as a child. I guess it's too expensive to travel across the world with someone who may or may not remember their experience when they're older. I must say, I do appreciate this experience more as an adult.

"Are you ready to go yet?" Hugh asks as he watches the television in the bedroom.

"Yes, just putting some perfume on and I'll be ready," I say, trying to look and smell wonderful in case I have to talk to Jessica.

"Okay, we can't be late," Hugh says to rush me out the door.

"Alright, alright. I'm ready!"

"You look beautiful, Scarlett."

"So do you, Hugh."

"Very funny."

I grab my purse and the room key as we walk out of this gorgeous place. I take one last glance with hopes of returning shortly to crawl back into bed. We make it to the elevator and Hugh tells me he's happy to be on this adventure with me and wouldn't want to do it with anyone else. I couldn't agree more. I'm so excited. Time to walk into the lion's den. Can't wait to see what's about to happen next.

# Nine

## Escar-NO

Have you ever walked into a room full of people where you immediately feel uncomfortable because everyone is staring at you and whispering like catty middle schoolers? That's the current situation Hugh and I are facing at this reception for everyone from *Hearst*. I don't recognize anyone from my side of the office, but, of course, I see Jessica standing in the corner with a few other girls, chatting and sipping their glasses of red wine. I can only imagine what they are discussing at this very moment.

There's a table with nametags as soon as you walk in the door of this huge conference-looking room with both of our names. Thank God. I was starting to wonder if they sent me here by mistake, or, even better, a joke. I place the white, square nametag on my chest right under my left shoulder. These stupid nametags never stay on when you want them to. I find them to be rather resourceful at events like this considering I don't know anyone except Hugh and that girl I won't mention again until I have to.

"Are we allowed to drink at this kind of event? I don't want to cross the line," I ask Hugh.

"Of course. Obviously just don't get hammered. Limit yourself to two glasses, I guess," Hugh replies quietly.

"I feel like that's fair. I just feel extremely uncomfortable right now. I don't really know what to do," I say while looking around the room hoping to find someone I know.

"I realize you feel like a fish out of water right now, but I assure you it will get better once you introduce yourself and mingle a bit," Hugh reassuringly says.

All of these roundtables have numbers on them. I guess that's why our nametags have numbers, too. Duh! Of course Hugh doesn't have the same number on his tag as me. I have a feeling there will be many situations, over the next few months, when we will be split up at these events. This is one of the nicer work events that I have attended since working at *Cosmo*. I feel like I'm at a wedding reception for someone I don't know. The servers are walking around, handing out heavy hors d'oeuvres to everyone, and I'm starting to realize that I'm starving since I skipped lunch today for a nap.

"Would you care for some, madam?" asks the server, wearing a white shirt and black pants.

"Umm... sure! Why not?" I say as I take the small mushroom-looking thing off the tray and put it on the napkin.

"Hugh, what is this? It's so slimy!" I ask with a disgusted look on my face.

"That's escargot, my love. Did you not know that?"

"*Eww!* Why would I know that? I just picked it up thinking it was a stuffed mushroom. Gross!" I say, spitting it into the napkin.

"Oh, boy. The wonders of France have already made an impression on you. They aren't for everyone. I don't care for them either. Try the croissant sandwiches. They should be a safe bet," Hugh says, grabbing one from a waiter's tray.

"Now this I can handle. Why can't they have normal food here? I'm so hungry," I say as I stuff my face with a cheese and ham croissant.

We both turn around to hear someone speaking over a microphone at the back of the room near a podium. Everyone starts walking toward the sound like a heard of sheep.

"Bonsoir, everyone! My name is Clark Green. I run the *Hearst* office here in Paris. So glad to have you here in Paris for the next few months! I know Fashion Week is not until the first week of March, but we have a lot to do leading up to that paramount event. I hope you are pleased with the hotel we have selected for you to stay in this weekend. We want you to know you have worked very hard to get this far, and we think you deserve this," announces Clark.

I'm looking around to see everyone gawking at this man. I guess he's kind of a big deal in the company – he's someone I need to suck up to in order to get sent home with a good recommendation or something. Clark looks to be about forty, if I had to guess, but it's hard to tell with men because I think they wear their age better than women sometimes.

"Tonight, we will mingle and get to know each other over a dinner we have planned for you. We have placed you at different tables at random so that you will branch out and meet people from all over the company. Tomorrow, you may do whatever you'd like until the evening when we will have another dinner with a special guest speaker," says Clark with a big smile on his face.

He probably knows how awkward this meal is about to be for all of us. I guess it won't be too bad since we all speak English, and we are probably all very hungry by now so we don't care who we're sitting next to. I don't really care what happens as long as they give me something recognizable to eat.

I briskly make my way to table seven, leaving Hugh and my comfort zone, with high hopes of not having to sit at the same table as Jessica. I'm the first one at my table, and I look over to Hugh's table at the front of the room and notice Jessica sitting at table one. When I said I didn't want her at my table, I meant I didn't want her at his either. I know I'm starting to look insecure, but I'm not. I'm just annoyed with her overall presence. I think she rubs me the wrong way because when I first met her all she could do was fawn over my boyfriend and act shocked when she found out I existed.

"Hi, my name is Trey. I work at *Marie Claire* as an editor for the relationship column," Trey says politely, extending his hand to shake mine.

"Hello, Trey. My name is Scarlett. I work at *Cosmo* as a fashion writer, and this is my first trip overseas," I say, trying to break the ice.

"Nice to meet you, Scarlett. Where are you from?" Trey asks as he put his napkin in his lap like a gentleman.

Now that I'm distracted, I'm not as concerned with what's happening at table one or anything else for that matter. I have to realize that this is a huge world I live in, and there are many kind people that would love to be my friend.

"I'm from Charleston, South Carolina. I attended College of Charleston where I graduated from last May." I think this is one of the first times I've been able to talk about my personal life at work without having to lie. "What about you?" I ask.

"That's right below me, surprisingly. I'm from Wake Forest, North Carolina. I went to Appalachian State University a few years back. I guess that gives my age away," Trey says with a giggle.

"My aunt went there. I have no idea how you could withstand that kind of cold. I have such thin, Southern blood. I don't think I'm fully prepared to endure the kind of cold we're about to experience here in France."

"After climbing up and down a mountain to get to class for four years, you get used to it. I think you'll like it here. This is my second year winning this contest, and I loved it last year."

Trey does look like a mountain man now that I think about it. He has the scruffy beard and Patagonia look that you see on the West Coast. I wouldn't say he's my type, but he's attractive enough. I don't care for facial hair, so he'd have to get rid of that before I could consider him a worthy candidate. Of course, I don't need a candidate because I'm happily tied down to Hugh. The rest of the group filed in and sat down at our table after a few minutes of conversing with Trey. I'm sure it's the jetlag, but I've been feeling a bit homesick already. I know my mind is somewhere else – that place being home where my family is suffering from the news of my grandmother. I can't stop wondering why she didn't tell me sooner. I'm upset they kept something so monumental from me, as if I couldn't handle it or something.

After learning everyone's name at the table, we are now well acquainted and the server is bringing us baskets full of warm, artisan bread. I can't wait to get my hands on this French bread – something I've been dreaming of since I found out I was coming here. I want to take the whole basket and put it on my plate. There are four girls, including me, and two guys at this table, so I'm glad I'm not outnumbered. I don't want to be "that girl" who stuffs her face with bread and butter, but I swear I could eat ten pieces right now. I don't really care what they think of me because I don't really need or care to impress them, but I don't want to make a terrible first impression on them, either. So, I take one piece and pretend I'm satisfied.

"Do you guys have any plans for tomorrow since we get the day to explore and do whatever we want?" I ask the table, being bold, trying to break the ice.

"I want to go shopping and go to the top of the Eiffel Tower," says Zoe, the cute Asian girl that works as a photographer at *Elle*. She's very petite with an eclectic style and huge glasses with tortoise frames. I don't think I could pull it off, but she's rocking it pretty well.

"I want to check out Sacre-Coeur because I hear it's a hidden gem of Paris and most tourists don't know to go there. I'm sure it's still going to be crowded, but I'm interested in checking it out," says Avery, the tall, athletic, soccer-looking chick sitting across from me. If she doesn't play sports, what a waste of height.

I'm starting to get the feeling a lot of the people here haven't been to Paris before. I sure haven't heard of Sacre-Coeur or whatever that place is. I'd like to check it out though. Maybe Hugh will take me tomorrow after a romantic lunch somewhere. After what seemed like a half an hour, we finally got a small salad that didn't look at all like the ones I get at home. This is just a bed of mangled looking lettuce and some weird vinegar dressing with shredded carrots on top.

"You're never going to escape these salads in France. This is the classic French salad that they serve everywhere in France. I usually just force it down because the meals take forever here and you'll be starving by the time you get your dinner," says Trey as he forces himself to eat his salad.

"Why do they insist on this dressing? It tastes so bitter and awful!" exclaims Miller, the guy who hasn't said two words this entire time.

•••

Finally, after nearly an hour of talking about our lives and what we expect from this trip, we receive our dinner. I cannot believe what they put in front of me – fish with the head still fully intact. Don't get me wrong, I love seafood. I just don't like to put a face with the fish I'm eating. I know this is something they do in Europe, because my dad warned me of this, but I wasn't expecting it on day one. I swear to God I will be skinny as a rail when I come home if I have to eat like this for the next few months. After trying to eat the edible parts of the fish, and eating the potatoes and vegetables on my plate, I'm hopeful for dessert. Of course that means we will have to be here another half hour because the service is so slow. I'm not trying to complain about the service, but I'm so exhausted, and I just want to go back to the room with Hugh to have some normalcy.

We waited for a short while, and I decided to ask for some wine while I waited for my dessert. I don't think I can handle much more of this without having some. I talk with the other girls about Hugh and how we met, and the guys kind of just sat there wishing they were at a table with less estrogen. I could tell that the girls knew exactly who Hugh was when I described him as the hot Australian photographer for *Harper's Bazaar*. I have a feeling Hugh might be more popular around the office than I was aware of. I glanced over at Hugh's table to see that he isn't engaged in any conversation with anyone. Instead, he's looking down at his phone. I know I have nothing to worry about with him. He's the perfect boyfriend and would never do anything to disrespect me.

After dessert, we all stood up and made small talk with each other trying to leave the table so we could get back to our rooms. I made my way to Hugh and begged him to take me back upstairs. Thankfully, he was very much on board with that idea. Tonight wasn't so bad, minus the fact that I'm still really hungry.

"Please tell me we can order room service and get something edible before we go to bed?" I ask Hugh.

"The escargot and fish head didn't satisfy you tonight, huh?" Hugh asks with a grin on his face.

"Ugh. I cannot eat French food if this is what it's going to be like for the next three months. Please tell me you can order me a steak or a burger with a large plate of fries," I say in a graveling tone of voice.

"That is something I can make happen. After all, it is called the "French-fry," he says while putting his arms around my neck.

"Ha ha, very funny. But really, let's make that happen, immediately."

# Ten

## Le Meilleur Jour: Part Un

I think I just slept for thirteen hours if I'm not mistaken. The sun is blinding me through the hotel drapes, and Hugh is still asleep despite how bright it is. After we returned last night, we had room service bring the most delicious burger I've had since Shake Shack before we left New York. Nothing can top Shake Shack, obviously, but it was a close second. We ate and cuddled in bed while watching some French movie that was on TV, and fell asleep shortly after. I know that sounds cheesy, but the older I get, the more I enjoy the little things in life. Yesterday was one of the longest days of my life, but I managed to survive it without falling apart too terribly.

The room category we're staying in features a complimentary car so you can tour Paris. Apparently, we are going to take full advantage of that today. You're supposed to have a driver take you, but somehow Hugh was able to persuade the hotel that he has a French driver's license even though I'm pretty sure he doesn't even have an American driver's license. There he goes again with his alluring ways. Allegedly, he has some kind of day planned for us where I need to dress "stylish" but comfortable. I'm not sure how I'm going to pull that off, considering my idea of comfortable is sweat pants and fur boots, but I'll manage to figure something out. I'm going to let Hugh sleep for a few more minutes so that I can check my emails to see what's going on back home. Sure enough, there's a note from my mom in my inbox:

Subject: I Miss You

*Dear Scarlett,*

*I can't even express how sorry I am for not telling you about your grandmother and for keeping something so huge from you. I truly hope you won't lose faith in me or resent me for my decision to withhold this from you. I was merely trying to protect you from the hurt and pain that I knew it would cause if you found out before your trip. I do hope you can forgive me, and know that I love you very much. Your grandmother is a strong woman, and she will make it through this with her head held high. The only thing she cares about is how she's going to look after treatment. She says that her and Jesus are "tight," and He won't let her lose her hair - HA! At least she still has a sense of humor. Anyway, I hope you are having the time of your life in Paris. Go check out Sacre-Coeur and get some pan au chocolate for me! I hope to hear from you and see some pictures soon.*

*Love Always,*
*Mama Bear <3*

Funny, I was just thinking that my grandmother would probably be concerned with her appearance after she receives the chemo treatments. I'm glad her spirits are lifted and she can laugh about things. Also funny that my mom suggested we go to Sacre-Coeur since Avery was suggesting that last night. I'm very curious as to what this place is all about considering the hype. Maybe Hugh will take me there soon. After perusing the Internet for pictures, I must say, it does look rather intriguing. I think we will probably stick to the more popular places today since I've never been here before, but I never know what to expect with Hugh.

I think I shall surprise Hugh with breakfast in the room so we won't have to go out to eat. I know this five-star hotel will have something we can enjoy. Let's hope.

"Yes, hello. This is room 6224 calling for room service," I politely say to the front desk.

"Bonjour, madam. What can we get for you today?" the woman asks with her broken English.

"I would like champagne, orange juice, the bread basket, assorted fruit, the breakfast meats, and the potatoes, please."

"We will have that up shortly, madam," she says, and hung up abruptly.

Now all I have to do is jump in the shower and hope the breakfast is here by the time I get out. I'm shocked that Hugh can sleep through all of this, but perhaps once I turn the shower on he will want to join me. I feel like this morning is getting off to a wonderful start. I just hope that the day continues on this path.

"Scarlett, I'm coming!" Hugh shouts from the other room.

"Come join me, my darling," I say from the side of the half glass door.

"I heard you earlier but didn't want to interrupt you from whatever it was that you were doing," says Hugh while kissing my neck.

"Is that what it was you were doing? I could have sworn you were snoozing the day away!" I say sarcastically.

"You caught me. I was exhausted. But I'm ready for the day to begin. I have some fun things on the itinerary today," Hugh says, pulling me in for more affection.

"Did you hear that?" I ask.

"I didn't hear anything. I'm in my own little world in here," Hugh says while grazing his fingers down my back.

"I think it was our room service being delivered," I say pulling away.

"You ordered room service? How romantic of you." Hugh apparently thinks I'm not the romantic type, but he will find out I'm capable. "It can wait. Come back here, you silly girl," Hugh says, grabbing my arm to pull me back in.

For the next ten minutes or so, we stayed in the shower to talk and do other things that I won't go into. I'm sure our food is cold by now, but I don't really care.

•••

Now time for breakfast. We enjoyed the wonderful French cuisine that wasn't too far off from an American breakfast, except for the fact that it wasn't the kind of meat I was expecting. I was hoping for the bacon or sausage that I'm used to at IHOP. Instead, they sent a plate of cold cuts and some weird meat I never saw before and wouldn't be able to identify if my life depended on it. I feel like I'm going to have a hard time figuring out what kind of food I like here. Hugh said he is going to help me order when we're out today.

"So, what *are* we doing today, babe?" I curiously ask while sipping my mimosa.

"Well, since we have the car, I thought we could drive around the city to my favorite spots. I was thinking we could start our day at the Louvre. Then, I will take you on a bike tour after lunch. This tour will show you a lot of the city you can't see in a car. Once we're done with that, I will take you for dessert at my favorite bakery in St. Germaine.

"That sounds like a busy day, but I'm excited! I hope we can do all of that. I know we have to be back at the hotel by eight tonight in order to hear that guest speaker."

"We will make it happen. It's still very early. Besides, I really only want to show you the Mona Lisa and a few other important pieces of art. You could spend a week in the Louvre and not see everything in its entirety. We can just go for a little while since you can't get lunch anywhere until noon, and the bike tour doesn't start until one thirty," Hugh says.

"Sounds perfect."

•••

We got ready for the day and made our way down to the lobby to get the keys to the car. I'm still in shock that they are letting us take this car out in the city where the driving is insane and we don't even have a French driver's license. After filling out the two-page insurance information, they handed us the keys and took us outside to the front of the hotel where the car is waiting.

"A Mini Cooper?" I ask in shock to the bellboy.

"Oui, madam."

"This should be fun to whip around the city," I say while trotting down the stairs to the car.

"Little cars drive faster than you think," Hugh says as he sat in the driver's seat.

"Oh, I'm sure you're going to prove that to me," I say as I fasten my seatbelt as tight as it will go to prove I'm scared of his driving.

"You don't have to worry. I had a car in Australia. I think I'm going to manage just fine, thank you very much," Hugh counters.

•••

As we pull away from the hotel in our black Mini Cooper, I look at Hugh with his fancy sunglasses, chic dark jeans, gray v-neck shirt, and his hand on the wheel and think this is probably going to be the best day ever. I can't even describe how tantalizing he is right now as he is taking command of the car and our day. I love when he takes control of the situation and I just sit back and relax knowing he will take care of me. I feel safe with Hugh. I don't feel safe in a boring way – I feel safe in the way that makes me feel comforted. I know that he will make me happy no matter what we do today.

I can't get enough people watching here. Everyone looks so different in Europe. I have yet to see a blonde-haired woman walking around the streets of Paris. I'm not saying that's a bad thing; it's just something I have noticed so far. I'm sure once we start working with the models at Fashion Week, I will see some familiar looking faces. I'm still curious as to what I will be doing for the magazine during my time here. I assume I will just be interviewing designers and writing about the current styles and trends. I'm hoping I won't just be sitting on the sidelines, watching and observing. I can't take a backseat to that kind of thing. I like to dip my feet in the water and get a feel for what I'm doing.

"We're almost at the Louvre. I just need to find a parking garage," Hugh exclaims.

"I'm just sitting over here taking it all in. Sorry for being quiet. I can't stop staring at the beautiful architecture and the people," I respond.

"I knew you'd be enticed by the city. I'm glad you're enjoying yourself," Hugh says while briefly taking his hand off the gearshift to place it on mine.

"Hey, Mister! Keep driving! I know it's hard to keep your hands off of me, but you can resist while you have precious cargo," I giggle.

"I think I know how to drive a stick shift, love. I've been driving since I was twelve years old."

"Oh, is that right? Well, I've been driving since then, too, if you qualify driving a boat as the same thing," I boast.

"I'll give you that because I like you. Can you drive a manual?" Hugh boasts back.

"Of course I can. My grandfather taught me on his old Jaguar in a parking lot when I was fifteen. I wouldn't say I'm good at it, but I know how."

After what seemed like a very long drive to this museum, we finally pull into this sketchy-looking parking garage. I've never in my life been in a parking garage that goes underground like this one does. Not to mention, the road is so narrow leading us down this windy path to the garage. I feel like I'm in a video game. I'm trying to keep it together, but I'm not thrilled with the height of this ceiling, the curvy road, and how tiny this garage is turning out to be.

"Stop panicking, Scarlett," Hugh reassures.

"It's hard for me to sit here wondering how you are making it down six levels of parking garage on this narrow-ass road. I don't get Europe," I respond with nervousness in my voice.

"This is how almost all of the parking garages are in Europe. They don't want garages on every corner. It would destroy the beauty of the city. Plus, it takes up too much space up there."

"I guess you have a point. I'm not a fan of them though. I'll have to get used to this."

I'm having a hard time adjusting to all of this change. I know I'm an adult and I'm supposed to adapt better, but I am really starting to miss home. I guess it will take time to get used to all the nuances in Paris. Now that we are eight floors below the street in this garage, we can finally find a parking space and get back to fresh air. I feel like I'm suffocating down here. You won't know what it's like until you experience it for the first time like I just did.

Hugh put his backpack on and locked the Mini Cooper. I put my belongings in the backpack so I won't have to carry a purse around all day. There's something freeing about not having to tote a bag around when you're exploring. My mom used to be the one who carried all of my stuff when we'd go to Disney World when I was a kid. I like feeling carefree like that today. I'm happy that I'm not the one in control for once. I do like having control, but sometimes it's nice when you feel taken care of like this. We took some of the snacks that I packed from home, and bottles of water from the room, so we wouldn't have to buy any while we're out today.

"I've never seen so many people exploring in one city besides New York," I say, looking around at all the tourists at the museum.

"You will always see tourists in Paris. People will be taking photos at this museum like you've never seen before," Hugh explains.

"I'm so excited to be here with you, babe! This place is incredible. I love the cobblestone ground and the tall buildings surrounding the Louvre."

"We probably need to get a photo of us in front of it, don't you think?" asks Hugh.

"I love that you want to take pictures with me. Of course we need one! I can't wait to post pictures for everyone to see back home.

We walk toward the front of the iconic glass pyramid to find someone willing to take our picture for us. There's a number of Asians here, with their very nice cameras, taking photos – maybe they will help us.

I politely ask one of the Asian men standing near us to take a photo of us. He didn't speak English, so I just handed him my phone and motioned for him to take one for us. He knew exactly what I was asking, so he stood about five feet away and started taking pictures of Hugh and I together. He returned my phone with a huge smile, and we look at the photos together.

"He did a great job," I say, flipping through the ten pictures he took on my IPhone.

"Yes, he did. I'm glad you aren't timid and you could ask him to do that for us," Hugh says.

"Let's go get in that line. We could be here a while," Hugh says, pointing at the line wrapped around the pyramid.

I was an art minor in college; however, I've never been super excited to go to a museum. I like museums, and I absolutely love the MET in New York City, but I can't see the hype of this place to stand in the cold for hours on end to get inside. It's not that cold today, but then again, I just might be getting used to the balmy air by now. There are so many people of different ages and ethnicities here. I've never seen such a melting pot of cultures in one place at the same time. Sure, I live in NYC, but you don't see this many different cultures at once. There are kids of all ages here, couples, and adults in large groups, too. I bet if I asked around, there would be people from South Carolina in this crowd. Hell, maybe even Australia if we asked.

"I want to take you to see some Monet, and, of course, The Mona Lisa. Then we can leave. I know you don't want to be stuck inside all day. I just thought you should get a feel for what this museum is all about," Hugh says while we edge closer to the front of the line.

"I'm excited to see what all the hype is about. I've wanted to come to this museum since I was old enough to know what it is."

•••

We make it to the front of the crowd and pay our fee to get in. So annoying that if we had come tomorrow, on Sunday, it would have been free. I can't imagine how long the line would have been on a day when the museum costs nothing. I don't think I'd want to be in that kind of crowd. Going down the stairs, we find our way to the Mona Lisa exhibit. Naturally, there are hundreds of people going in the same direction. Hugh told me that the last time he was here, someone got arrested for trying to touch the glass case the painting is in. I can't imagine being stupid enough to try and touch the artwork at a museum, especially not something as famous as the Mona Lisa. I still don't see why people get so excited and worked up about a piece of art.

"Here she is," Hugh says, pointing towards the painting.

"That's it?" I'm not supposed to act like a brat, but this is stupid. "It's not as big as I anticipated it to be."

"Yep. There it is. Her eyes are moving if you pay close enough attention," Hugh says.

"How can you tell? I don't think that's true. I don't notice her doing anything to me," I say annoyed.

"I think you're supposed to pretend. Who knows?" Hugh responds.

"Whatever. This is silly. I guess you should take a picture of me in front of this so my parents can see."

"Yes, stand in front, as close as you can get," Hugh says while pulling out the phone to take a picture of me.

I feel silly having my picture taken in front of a piece of artwork that didn't impress me very much. I know this should amaze me, but I'm not seeing it. I love Monet, but I can't get into this. After taking the picture through the sea of people, I suggest we move on to a section of the museum that's less crowded. I can't stand being in a crowd of slow walking people in a place like this. I'm trying hard to stay positive, but I'm getting a little anxious.

"Stop worrying, babe. We will be out of here in a minute," Hugh says.

"I know. I just want to go where we can have some space to breath," I say.

"I don't think I've ever been here when it's quite this crowded," Hugh remarks.

"I don't see how people can truly enjoy the artwork when you're getting stepped on and shoved out of the way," I say.

"I get what you're saying. Let's go find somewhere more peaceful," Hugh says.

# Eleven

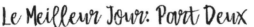

## Le Meilleur Jour: Part Deux

When I decided to minor in art at C of C, I had no idea how many specific classes I would have to take to fulfill my degree. One of those obscure classes was sculpture – something I knew I probably would not be very good at and probably would never do again after I graduate. Well, it was either sculpture or history of prehistoric art – there was obviously no contest there. What I'm getting at is, during my senior year, I had to create a popular piece recognizable to those who are not art majors. After flipping through my underutilized, expensive textbooks, I found Michelangelo's "Dying Slave" and decided that everyone would recognize this. How could they not? Well, too bad when I created my version, nobody could recognize it, except for the *anatomy* if you know what I mean. I ended up getting a C+ since I was able to make my class laugh for nearly twenty minutes during my presentation and for the overall effort. My teacher said I disgraced one of the most beautiful works of art.

Part of the reason I chose that particular piece of art was the meaning behind it. I felt agony every single time I had to analyze and shape together the slave's body or thought about the plight of slavery. I will forever have the upmost respect for sculptors.

"I want to go see this sculpture I tried to recreate in my class last year," I say to Hugh, hoping he won't ask why.

"Okay, let's go check it out, then we have to go get ready for our bike tour," Hugh says while looking at the map of the Louvre. This place is a freaking maze.

•••

After walking through the tall corridors of the Louvre, and up the stairs to the exhibit, we made our way to the sculpture.

"Wow, mine wasn't too far off... Just kidding! This looks nothing like mine. I wasn't going to tell you because I'm embarrassed that you're great at everything you do and I tend to be average at everything that I do."

"I don't think many could recreate this, Scarlett. I don't think you're average at anything. I think you're amazing in every way. Why are you so hard on yourself?"

"Because. I'm a female in my early twenties, and that's what we do. I'm thankful you see me differently. It's like you have permanent blinders on and you only see the good in me."

"Maybe I do," Hugh says while grabbing my shoulders behind me and kissing my left cheek.

•••

Something about being in this museum makes me feel insignificant. It's probably the fact that I'm surrounded by all of these incredible pieces of art. Sadly, almost all of these people were dead when they became famous. If I ever become famous after I'm dead, I'm going to be pissed from up above. I want recognition while I'm alive. I doubt I'll ever do anything noteworthy enough to become that kind of famous. I don't see how people spend hours on end just staring at artwork. My eyes feel heavy, and I'm hungrier by the minute as we walk around this place.

I turn to Hugh and look at him with my eyebrows furrowed. "Is that Miller over there sitting on that bench?"

"That skinny, light-skinned black guy over there?" Hugh asks as he subtly points to our three o'clock view.

"Yes. He was sitting at my round table last night and barely said two words to us," I say in a whisper so he doesn't hear us.

"Should we speak to him you think?" Hugh asks.

"I mean, if we're in a hurry, maybe not. But then again, I'd feel bad if he saw us and we avoided him."

Miller is the type of guy I always wanted to rescue in middle school for being the outcast of the group. I usually befriended this type of person in hopes to make their day a little better. Middle school is a nightmare to begin with, much less when you're a loser who plays the trumpet in the band and eats alone at lunch. Part of me thinks I did it because I felt like an outcast, too. Middle school was a hard time for me because my parents were separated, and I was old enough to know what was going on, but Savannah had no clue. I was constantly lying to her about where my dad was in order to keep things under wraps. I feel like I should try to see what Miller is doing here alone so I can enjoy the rest of the afternoon without feeling like a dark cloud is looming over my head.

I walk toward the bench Miller is sitting at and try to tap his shoulder without alarming him too much.

"Miller, hi. It's Scarlett, from last night," I say in hopes he will remember so I don't feel more awkward than I already do.

"Oh my gosh, you startled me! Wow, hi, Scarlett. Who are you here with?" Miller asks politely.

"Miller, this is my boyfriend, Hugh Hamilton. We were just about to leave to go on a bike tour of the city," I say, realizing that he might be upset he's all alone and we have fun plans.

"Hi, Hugh. Nice to meet you. I hope you two have fun. I hear those tours are a great way to see Paris," Miller says as he clasps his hands together.

I look at Hugh, and he looks back at me with the "go ahead, Scarlett" look on his face. I hate to ruin the perfect day that Hugh has planned for us, but I could be working with this guy a lot while I'm here and need him later on.

"Miller, how would you like to join us for the tour? I'm sure they can squeeze you in last minute," I ask.

"Oh, no, I couldn't be an imposition," Miller responds.

"You're not an imposition. Come with us, man. It will be a good time," Hugh cajoles.

I'm lucky that Hugh is the type of guy who sees kindness as an important personality trait. Most guys would be pissed that I invited another man on our date. Hugh seems to be on the same page as me. Either way, I feel better knowing Miller won't be alone the rest of the afternoon. You should have seen the look on Miller's face when Hugh reassured him to join us. It was priceless, and it made us both feel so happy knowing we made someone's day. If there's something I've learned from growing up in the South, it's be kinder than necessary to everyone because you never know the battle they might be facing.

•••

The three of us got in a cab to head to the bike tour place by the Eiffel Tower. We decided to leave the car in the garage in case there wasn't any nearby parking. This is my first experience in a French cab, and I must say it's not as bad as the ones in New York. I guess I thought they'd be filthy for whatever reason. Maybe someone told me that France isn't that clean or that they don't maintain their buildings that well.

"Miller, where are you from? Are you excited to be in Paris?" I had to say something because I don't do well with silence. It's awkward.

"I'm from Brooklyn, originally, and I went to NYU for journalism. Of course I'm excited. This is my first time coming here. I graduated from college when I was nineteen because I was home-schooled all my life. I ended up starting school early and graduating from college super young. I interned for *Vogue* for a while and got tired of being the errand boy. Luckily, *Cosmo* took a chance on me."

"You work for *Cosmo*? How have I never seen you on our side of the office?" I ask.

"Probably because you weren't looking. I see you every day at work! I feel bad I haven't introduced myself before now. As you can infer by now, I'm not much of a social butterfly."

"I work for *Harper's Bazaar,* and I've never seen you either, but my office isn't as close, so I have an excuse. I'm glad you're going with us so Scarlett can have another friend at work," Hugh replies.

"Absolutely. I usually work through lunch and sit at my desk. I'm still living at home, so my mom packs my lunch like I'm in elementary school. I can't complain – it saves me a ton of money," Miller says, laughing at himself.

"Hey, nothing to be ashamed of there. I lived with my parents until I moved to New York back in October. There's something to be said for not having to go to the grocery store or do your laundry. Although I ended up doing those things for myself when I got out of school."

"Can we change the subject? You two are making me feel ANCIENT," Hugh exclaims.

•••

We are finally at Fat Tire Bike Tours, and we are looking around to see what this place is all about. It's a small building with round tables inside and t-shirts for sale. There are bikes inside, and Segways in here for whatever reason. I guess they do other types of tours around the city besides bikes. Outside, there is a gravel lot that has about 100 red bikes neatly lined up in a few rows. There's one thing that stands out the most about this – everyone here is speaking English. Thank you, Lord, for letting my ears hear my native tongue. I know this sounds weird, but I feel like home here. I feel like I'm at a bike shop back in America. Everyone is standing around in little groups, chatting about their site seeing and what district they're staying in. Hugh checked us in and added Miller to the tour group we are in for 2:00 p.m. today.

"Hello, everybody. If you can meet me outside to get fitted for your bike, and to get put into your group, that would be great," announces one of the several tour guides.

We walk outside, and I realize that I haven't been on a bike since college when I would ride around campus from classes. Let's just say I'm not in as good of shape as I was then, and I'm a bit nervous about riding around a city I know very little about. My balancing skills are about to be put to the test.

"This isn't so hard! These bikes ride like a dream," I say to Hugh and Miller.

"I've never been on a bike, so this should be interesting!" Miller laughs.

"What! Are you kidding me? How do you plan on doing this tour if you've never been on a bike?" I ask shocked.

"I'm pretty sure I've seen enough people do it to get the idea," Miller says with confidence.

"Just be careful. I might get fired if they find out you were injured while flitting around Paris with me," I say, tying my shoelaces extra tight.

•••

Valentine is the name of our instructor who will be guiding us around the city. Never in my life have I heard of a man named Valentine, but I guess it's a popular name where he comes from. He says he's from Romania and he's here to take a break from school. He can't be much older than Hugh if I had to guess. He's a friendly guy, very short and cute, and the girls in our group seem to think so as well. To my surprise, Miller seems to be doing fine on his bike as I watch from the side. Hugh is riding closely behind him to make sure he doesn't fall. I still can't believe he's never been on a bike. I guess when you grow up in a big city there aren't many places to learn. Hugh was raised in the suburbs like I was, so, of course he knows how to ride a bike.

The city does look different on a bike than it does in the car or just walking around. There's something very liberating about riding around the city, going from landmark to landmark, seeing things this way. I'm enjoying it very much, and I didn't expect to. I knew Hugh would not have planned something if he didn't think I would like it. He said he's been on many bike tours around the city and the night tour is the best one. He said we could go in a few weeks if we want to since they show you another side of the city and you get to go on a boat tour on the Seine.

After our two-hour tour of Paris, and many photos later, Hugh and I are now alone and can finally have some privacy at the café he wanted to take me to. Miller was pretty worn out after that ten-mile bike ride and wanted to take a nap before we have to go to the guest speaker later.

"This place has an incredible view of the Eiffel Tower, babe. Thanks for bringing me here," I say, putting my hand on top of his.

"I'm glad you're impressed. It's the best view and the best steak and fries the whole city has to offer," he smiles back at me with confidence in his decision to bring me here.

•••

He wasn't wrong. That was the best steak and fries I ever had, not to mention the best glass of red wine I ever had, too. I feel like today was very successful, and I saw and learned a lot about Paris. I got to visit the Arc De Triumph, without getting run over by the crazy cars in the roundabout, the Tuileries Gardens, Napoléon's Tomb, and we ended up back at the Louvre, which worked out swimmingly for us to get our car back from the parking garage. Overall, today was a really good time, and I'm way more excited to be here than I was at first. I'm finally not thinking about work, family, stress, or anything. It has been the perfect day.

# Twelve

## Dear Diary

Let me take a moment to catch you up on my life from the past two weeks. Where do I start? Okay, so, the first thing that stands out as most important is living situations. After the bike tour and lunch at the café by the Eiffel Tower, we went back to The Peninsula Hotel for the guest speaker who turned out to be Christian Louboutin – famous for those beautiful shoes with the shiny *red* bottoms. Too bad he wasn't there to give any away but to talk about how he became one of the most famous French designers to date. After he left, we were given information about our living arrangements. I knew it was only a matter of time before I had to leave my dreamland hotel and Hugh sleeping in the same bed as me.

We had one last magical night together at the Peninsula, then reality hit: living with another chick. They told us we would all be living in the same building, and we would be close to where most of Paris Fashion Week would be held. That way, we could walk everywhere we needed to go. Surprisingly, the apartment building is fairly nice, and the loft I share with Zoe isn't so bad. Yep, I room with that spunky Asian chick that has more moxie than I predicted. I really enjoy her to be honest. I wasn't sure I'd like living with someone who is opposite of myself, but she's taught me a few things about fashion that I didn't know before. Mostly, you should just be yourself. She's the type of girl who wears a jean skirt with black fishnet tights underneath and a crop top in the wintertime. I don't think I'll go to that extreme, but I need to stop shopping at such traditional places. She likes to get her clothes from thrift stores and dress with a vintage flare.

Hugh ended up rooming with Trey, the mountain man from Wake Forest, believe it or not. I don't know how he got put with someone at my table, but I'm not mad about it. They live on the first floor, which is funny to me since I now live above him instead of below him like I did in NYC. To our surprise, Trey and Zoe seem to get along quite nicely. We keep telling them that they would be a cute couple and they should try to go out on a date. I don't think either of them listened, but they really might be the perfect yin and yang. It's usually those types of people that end up matching up just perfectly. I've tried to tell Zoe that she'd really like Trey if she would give him the time of day. I think he's more into her than she is into him. I'm starting to wonder if Zoe even likes the opposite sex. I haven't cracked her code yet – it's only been two weeks, mind you.

Besides our living arrangements, Courtney gave me tasks, via email, during my time here in Paris. She sent a long list of things she wanted me to do while here, and I started doing those things. She wants me to find designers and models to interview during PFW to see what a day in the life of the industry is like. On a daily basis, I've been gathering questions to ask when it happens this upcoming week. Yes, Fashion Week starts on February 1st, and I have little to no time to finish up these questions. To make things more pressing, Hugh has decided he wants to take me on a surprise little "holiday", as he calls it, before the craziness happens. That just about sums it up.

•••

"I know it sucks, but we won't get to spend much time celebrating your birthday and Valentine's Day since they are right before Fashion Week," Hugh says while sitting on my twin bed in the loft.

"Well, that's okay. We can just celebrate this weekend and make the most of it."

"We have the weekend off. Why don't I take you somewhere? Let's get out of this city and go explore."

"What did you have in mind, Mr. Money Bags?"

"Well, we can go somewhere nice without it costing an arm and a leg. Just consider it a Valentine's Day/birthday gift from yours truly."

"A combined trip, huh? Okay, I guess that works for me. As long as you don't plan on combining the gifts! HA!"

"I wasn't planning on doing that, missy. I shopped around for your birthday gift the other day while you were having dinner with Zoe and Trey."

"Is that right? You think you're sneaky, don't you?"

"Well, yes. It's much easier to hide your gifts now that we don't live in the same apartment. I thought I could *surprise* you with the destination. I've always wanted to do that. This is somewhere I've never been, but I've always dreamt about."

"How do you plan on keeping that a secret?"

"How about you just let me figure that out. Okay?"

"Ok… but if we are going somewhere, you need to figure it out fast since tomorrow is Friday!"

"Once I go back to my loft, I'll book it. I'll text you with the time and tell you the kind of clothes to pack. Better yet, I'll tell Zoe. Wait. No. She will have you looking like someone I don't recognize."

"You should leave the packing to me. I will figure it out. If I don't pack the right stuff, you can just take me shopping."

"Okay, deal."

Now that my wheels are spinning, and I have no idea where we're headed, I start to freak out a little bit. If you don't know this by now, I'm a bit of a control freak. I don't like not knowing what's going to happen. I've been using a planner since the 5th grade, and I don't plan on stopping until the day I die. I don't know why I'm like this, but I am. When people put "extremely organized" on their resume, and they don't mean it, it makes people like me really pissed. It's at the top of my qualifications.

Hugh:

9:32 p.m.

> *Hello, gorgeous. Trip is booked! I need you to meet me out front of our building with your suitcase at 5:30 a.m. sharp tomorrow. I know it's early, but it'll give us the whole day to explore the city. Plus, we have to train into the city. I don't think I can get us a cab or a car that early. Sorry for that.*

Me:

9:35 p.m.

> *Hi, handsome. Thank you for doing this for me. I feel really, really special. I don't mind waking up early. I'm too excited to sleep! What am I supposed to pack?*

Hugh:

9:42 p.m.

> *Sorry for that delay. Trey was suggesting things for us to do when we get there. He hasn't even been. That guy is such a funny individual. Anyways... I need you to pack layers. You won't need a heavy coat where we're going. That's the biggest hint I'll give you!*

Me:

9:44 p.m.

> *I sense there might be a temperature increase where we're going. You truly know the way to my heart, Hugh Hamilton <3*

Hugh:

9:45 p.m.

> *Goodnight, Scarlett Hanes. I love you. Sleep well!*

Me:

9:46 p.m.

*Goodnight! I love you more. Sweet dreams.*

•••

As if I didn't have the best boyfriend in the world before now, Hugh goes and wins me over once again with his charm. I can't believe I'm going on a mystery trip this weekend. Before I fall asleep, I email my mom and let her know I'll be away from Paris for the weekend, and if she must know details to contact Hugh. I made her promise not to tell me if she finds out before I do.

Oh, and one more thing I forgot to mention while I was telling you about the past few weeks… Addison and Claire are coming to visit March 1st during Paris Fashion Week so they can get to attend some of the events. Addison gets a spring break in law school, so she's taking that week to come here with her sister. Since I'm an employee of *Hearst Magazines*, I get VIP passes to a lot of the shows. I'm so excited to see them and to show them around Paris. Okay, good night for now.

# Thirteen

## It's More Than "Nice"

As you could suspect, I didn't sleep very well last night. I probably burned more calories switching sides to sleep on than I did walking to breakfast yesterday. I don't think that would have changed even if I knew where I was going today. I'm not one to rest well prior to a major event for whatever reason. I also can't eat anything this early in the morning. I had to wake up at four just to take a shower. Poor Zoe had to wake up as well since our place is so small, and the hair dryer sounds like a plane on a tarmac when you turn it on. Luckily for me, she's an early riser. That's actually the only lucky thing today. The other days it *really* annoys me.

It's a balmy thirty-six degrees this morning, and I had no idea what to wear, so I'll probably freeze. I figure I'll be inside mostly until we arrive at our final destination so I won't be cold unless I'm outside for longer than ten minutes.

"Good morning, beautiful," Hugh says after kissing me in the tiny lobby of our building.

"Good morning, babe. I'm so anxious to find out where we're going. It's killing me!"

"You'll know soon enough." Hugh never divulges any secrets when he has these kinds of plans. I have never once guessed a gift or anything he's planned since dating. "We need to walk down to the metro station to get to the REN station. That's where we will go to get to CDG airport," Hugh confirmed.

"Fine. Ugh!" I knew he wouldn't give me any ideas or hints. "Well, I hope it's not very far. I'm going to freeze if it is."

"I'll warm you up when we get to the train. I promise."

•••

After a short, four-minute walk to the train station, we are finally underground. I might add that we live in St. Germaine, one of the coolest places in Paris, if I must say. I love living here. I heard about it before I got here, so I knew it would be the happening place. It's in walking distance to the best shopping, restaurants, and the *Hearst Magazines* office space we're using to work out of while we're here.

"You were right. It's really warm down here," I say while taking off my sweater. It feels like a furnace is burning my skin.

"Told ya. Now we just have to get on the proper train to get us to the REN. Then we can take a short cab ride from there to the airport."

"Couldn't we just train the entire way? Save some money perhaps?"

"I don't suppose why not. We will have to be mindful of the time. Our flight departs at seven forty-five, so we'll determine that when we reach the REN station," Hugh says as he looks up from his glasses to glance at me.

Hugh hardly ever wears glasses, but when he does, oh my God. It's the hottest thing. I wish he'd wear them more often, but I guess he only wears them when he needs to see up close. I see him trying to order at restaurants without them and it's super funny to me. He said it's uncommon to lose up-close vision at his young age, but it happened about a year ago. He's wearing them right now so he can read the maps on his phone for the metro schedule. I love when he takes command of the situation. It's so sexy to me when a man is in control. Not to mention I have no idea how to read these French names for the stations, so he's got that under control for us.

After several stops on the train, we finally made it to the REN station where we will get on another train to take us to the airport. It only took about twenty-five minutes to get here, and it won't be too long on this train, either. Hopefully, we will make it on time, but we aren't checking any luggage so it won't be that big of a deal if we cut it close. It wouldn't be the first time I showed up late for a flight. I'm notorious for being on time for almost everything in my life except the airport, mostly because I'm not the one driving myself; I usually rely on my parents or whomever is taking me for my trip.

•••

"Okay, Scarlett. I'm going to get our tickets, and you cannot look at them when we pass them to the TSA agent with our passports. Got it?"

"Got it." I laugh a little because I know I'm going to want to peak. "What's my punishment if I look?"

"A good ass spankin, and no hugs or kisses for the duration of our trip," Hugh says seriously.

"I'm fine with the ass spanking, but you can't withhold the others," I say.

"You're pushing the envelope! Just let the surprise unfold. You'll be happier if you do."

I guess he's right. I need to just let him surprise me and see what happens. After all, this is the first time I've ever been on a mystery destination trip. We make our way through security, and I still don't know where we're headed. Hugh makes us sit at another gate nearby and won't let me look at the screens. I'm having a hard time not peaking over my shoulder to see what the screen says.

It's time to get on our flight, and Hugh makes me put on the noise cancelling headphones.

"You have to wear these the entire time. I know it's annoying, but that's the only way to ensure you don't find out where we're going until we get there."

"I don't mind. I'm totally down for this surprise. I promise."

"Good. Thank you for complying with the ridiculousness. I want this to be special for you."

Every single time Hugh does something romantic these days, I think he's going to pull out a ring and propose. I don't know why I think that. We've only been together for six months. I guess, to him, that's longer since he will be turning thirty this September. I don't know that I'm ready for marriage yet, but I guess by the time we're engaged for a while I would be ready. I'm not saying I haven't thought about it or planned it out in my head, because I have. Problem is, the woman never gets much say on the timeline of events – that stupid timeline of when the proposal will actually happen. I try not to bring up proposals or weddings to Hugh because I know that just makes a guy push back the date even further. It's hard for me to play it close to the vest, but I know it will increase the odds of getting engaged if I don't say anything.

•••

That didn't seem like a very long flight at all. Non-stop flights will forever hold a special place in my heart. I'm looking around, outside the little window on the plane, and I still can't seem to figure out where we are. Like I've said before a million times, all airports look the same to me. Rarely do they ever give away where you are, except for when I was in Hawaii. I knew where we were because there was water nearby. I don't see any water here, but it could be close if the temperatures are warmer like Hugh mentioned.

"We have to go quickly because I've arranged for a car to take us to the hotel, and they are to pick us up at the arrivals in fifteen minutes," Hugh says as he pulls our luggage down from the overhead bin.

"I can walk super fast if you hadn't figured that out by now. DUH."

"Good girl."

We walked briskly to the arrivals so that we could make our departure time of 9:30 this morning. I didn't even have time to look around to figure out where we might be. Part of me really wants to be surprised. The other part of me *really* wants to know where we are.

Finally, we made it to the outside of the airport where the black town car is waiting for us and the driver is holding up a sign that says "Hamilton" in bold black letters. It's kind of weird thinking about the fact that Hamilton could be my new last name soon. I'm sure my mom will be excited that my monogram wouldn't have to change too much. Those are the kinds of things she thinks of, sadly.

"Sorry we're a few minutes late. We're finally here and ready to go," Hugh says to the driver.

"We should be there in about thirty minutes," says the driver as he punches in the address into his GPS.

"Have you two ever been to Monaco?"

"MONACO?" I shout.

"Surprise!" Hugh says as he squeezes my thigh in the back seat.

"No, we've never been. We're very excited," Hugh says to the driver.

I can't believe I'm going to Monaco! That means we must be in Nice right now, and we will be driving down to the little country of Monaco to spend a romantic getaway. I can't wait to see what Hugh has planned for us this weekend.

# Fourteen

## Down by the Bay

This is quite possibly the most beautiful drive I've ever been on in my entire life. The views from the inside of this car are breathtaking and I can't even really see everything. We're about five minutes away from our hotel, and I can already see crystal blue water. We're staying at the Monte Carlo Bay Hotel Resort, which is right on the water. Apparently, it's a rather lavish hotel. I wouldn't expect anything different from my Prince Charming.

This hotel is really close to all the landmarks and fun places to go shopping and eat dinner. Hugh says we are going to spend the day touring the city and eating everything we can, specifically the seafood, which I have missed terribly since I don't live in Charleston anymore. I can't wait to eat some fresh lobster and shrimp while I'm here! I've never been to a casino before, so that should be fun as well. My grandmother used to go on cruises with her debutant society friends, and they would gamble and come home with little to no money afterward. Therefore, I've never been a big fan of wasting my money on such a risky thing. I'd like to see how everything goes down at a casino, but I might just be a spectator.

"We have arrived to your hotel," the driver says cordially.

"Great, merci beaucoup!" Hugh responds.

"Merci!" I say, chiming in like it even matters.

I can't stop looking around this place. The entrance of this hotel has tall columns, a big fountain in front of the entrance, and concierge waiting to help with luggage. This looks like the kind of place that waits on your every need and treats you like royalty. I love seeing the palm trees everywhere; I feel like I'm in paradise. I don't want to get in the way of the check-in process, so I walk over to the side of the circular driveway area to the ledge and see the water, the ocean – my favorite place in the world. The one place where I feel like time stands still and there is no chaos in my life. I snap a few pictures to send to my family and put it in an email so I can let them know where I ended up for the weekend with Hugh. I'm sure my mom has been on pins and needles wondering where her child was going to be for the next couple of days.

*Dear lovely family,*

*I never imagined I would be sending you pictures from Monaco, but here I am. This place is stunning and you would love it, no doubt. I hope everything is good in your world. I miss you SO much, and I hope to hear from you soon.*

*All my love,*
*Scar <3*

I think it's important for them to know what I'm up to while I'm here. I know that they wonder what I'm doing in Europe while their lives aren't changing very much at home. I worry about the health of my grandmother, and how she's feeling, all the time. I can only hope that she will be well again soon so maybe one day we can travel to a beautiful paradise like this together. I wish they wouldn't keep me in the dark so much considering I'm an adult who can handle things better than they know. Savannah isn't giving me any details, but she probably doesn't understand much of what's going on.

"Scarlett, our room is ready, babe," Hugh shouts from the entrance of the lobby.

"I'm coming!"

I run to the front to catch up with Hugh, and I realize it's much warmer here than it is in Paris. I shrug my jacket off and throw it over my shoulder. I hope I packed properly for this little getaway.

"This place is breathtaking! I can't even describe how I feel right now," I say to Hugh as we walk to the elevators.

"I was hoping you'd like it! I had a good feeling that you'd like somewhere that felt like home. This resort has sea salt air coming in from every angle. I can't wait to explore with you this weekend," Hugh says, kissing my cheek.

"I love it. I love you!"

We make our way to our hotel room on the ninth floor, and we find ourselves looking out at the ocean and the most beautiful views you could ever imagine.

"Oh my gosh! This is incredible. How did you find this place?"

"I just did a little research and found it to be the best view and close to everything. I wanted you to be able to clear your mind before Fashion Week and your friends coming into the city."

"You did a great job. My mind is only with you, here, in this hotel room."

There's nothing better than a huge, king-size bed with white linens and fluffy pillows. The bathroom is spa-like and has all of the amenities you need to enjoy your experience.

"I think we should get lunch down by the pool," Hugh says as he puts on his hat and slips into something cooler.

"Just let me freshen up a bit and we can go down there," I say from the bathroom as I wash my face.

•••

If you were wondering what adult Disneyland looks like, it's this resort. The pools and the grounds are impeccably landscaped and groomed, and the views span all around the city. Monaco isn't a very big place, and you can get to wherever you want to go by walking or taking a short taxi ride into the city center. I feel like I am about to order a drink with a little pink umbrella with a cherry and an orange inside. I need to get this vacation started the right way. It's not warm enough to swim in the ocean, or in the pool for that matter, but there is an indoor, heated pool that we might have to explore later tonight.

"The restaurant in the resort is top-notch, and that's where I want to take you to tonight," says Hugh while holding the lunch menu.

"What about going off the resort for dinner?"

"You won't want to. This chef has won a Michelin Star for his culinary expertise. I know you know all about that coveted award being the little chef that you are."

"Are you kidding me? I've dreamt of going to a Michelin-Star restaurant since I was ten years old. You have no idea how much that excites me!"

"I knew it would excite you. That's why I figured we'd just stay here tonight. We can go out tomorrow night and check out a casino if that sounds good to you."

"Sounds great. I'm just happy to be here with you and not think about work for a while."

•••

For lunch, we ordered fresh seafood and some cocktails while looking out at the ocean. Hugh and I talked about our future and what we want from our lives. Believe it or not, Hugh would like to settle down somewhere in a smaller city and start a family within the next few years. I shared my dream of one day owning a clothing boutique on King Street – farfetched, I know. That's always been a pipe dream of mine considering it would cost an arm and a leg to rent on King Street. All of the shopping worth going to in Charleston is on King Street. I guess if I worked hard enough, and we combined our skills, we could make it happen. Hugh wants to start his own photography company possibly working as a wedding photographer – something I wouldn't have seen him doing, but I know he would be great.

After lunch, Hugh and I walked around the resort to become acquainted with our surroundings a little before deciding on what to do this afternoon. Since it's the weekend before my birthday and Valentine's Day, Hugh decided it might be a good idea to go shopping for a special, birthday girl surprise. I don't hate the sound of that at all. It's always been interesting having my birthday two days after Valentine's Day because if a boy ever did something for me on Valentine's, he always felt he didn't have to celebrate my birthday two days later or give me another gift for that matter. Hugh is making sure that I am celebrated on both special days.

# Fifteen
## Poker Face

I never imagined myself owning a Chanel handbag, but here I am in the Chanel store holding one in my hands right now. This is something I pictured myself having one day when I'm thirty or when I have kids that are in middle school. I wouldn't have guessed that I'd be receiving one as a gift from my boyfriend for my twenty-third birthday. Of course, I selected a classic, iconic Chanel bag – one that everyone would recognize as soon as they saw it in the flesh. Black lambskin quilted leather with the silver medal Chanel symbol on the front – something a girl dreams of when she is into fashion the way I am. This purse will never go out of style, and I will never stop carrying it even if it does.

"Why do you spoil me so much, Mr. Hamilton?"

"You're easy to spoil. You might have expensive and exquisite taste, but you know what you like and you don't over think things – something refreshing I have never experienced with a woman before."

"Well, thank you! I definitely know what I like… *you* being one of those things."

"I'm glad you like me. I couldn't be happier celebrating your life on this planet for twenty-three years. I know your birthday isn't for another week, but I wanted to celebrate this weekend. We will be busy for the next two weeks. You have no idea what you're about to be in for with Fashion Week. *Cosmo* is going to work you like you've never been worked before."

"Game on, *Cosmo*. I'm ready."

"That's the spirit. You're tough. You can handle anything that comes your way. Now that you have this beautiful handbag, you can conquer the world."

"That's how I feel, for sure. I can't believe I'm actually carrying a designer bag. A *real* designer bag."

"Believe it, because you are. Just take good care of it and don't lose it. We might have to get this thing insured once we get home."

"Good plan."

•••

The day was well spent – shopping around Monaco and visiting some of the main attractions. It still doesn't feel right that I'm carrying this beautiful purse, but I'm sure it won't take long to get accustomed to. I'm starting to feel like a princess – a fat princess considering how much I've already eaten. Tonight, we are going to the Michelin-Star restaurant and taking it easy so we can be rested for tomorrow. I don't know what Hugh has in mind for us, but he says it will be fun and I have to wait and see. I thought the surprises were over, but I forget that Hugh always has something up his sleeve.

Luckily, I packed something fancy for going out at night because these restaurants don't let you in without looking a certain way. Hugh is wearing a dinner coat with a button down and dress pants, and I'm wearing a long-sleeved, silver-shimmery dress I got for New Years when I was in college. I'm shocked that I can still fit into this dress, but super happy nonetheless. I want to get a picture of us together to post on my social media.

"Excusez-moi," I say, asking the concierge to take a photo of us in the lobby. I held up my phone and asked for a picture. He knew what I was asking.

I don't know how, but this is one of the best pictures that we've ever had. The guy only took one picture because I don't think he knew I wanted options, but he did a good job. I'll have to post this immediately because I've never felt more confident in my life. I have my handsome boyfriend, and we're in this romantic resort, and I have my new, beautiful Chanel bag. Life can't get better than this.

•••

That was the best dinner I've ever had. I will say, the five-course meal has its perks when you want to try a little of everything. I thought the portions would be tiny, but they weren't too bad. Even though I didn't know half the things I was ordering, it showed up looking like normal American food. They aren't joking around with the prices at this place. I guess when you're eating some of the best cuisine in the world, you have to charge more than the usual upscale restaurant fees.

"It's time to go into the city and see what kind of poker face you can put on at the casinos," Hugh says as he gets up from the table.

"*Poker face*? Are you kidding me? My dad is a detective, honey. He taught me how to have a solid poker face when I was old enough to understand the meaning. You just wait, Mister!"

"Is that right?"

"Yes. In fact, it is."

"Very cute. Can't wait."

•••

I was expecting something bright and vibrant like the casinos on "The Hangover", but it's not like that here. It's upscale and bougie without the tacky crap you see in Vegas. Everyone is dressed impeccably here. In fact, I feel kind of underdressed. I guess we didn't get the memo that you should be wearing a tux and a floor length gown. If we had known that, I would have brought one. I guess they don't mind since they let us in. Not to mention, they probably don't care that much since it's off-season and we have money to blow at their casino.

"I want to go to the blackjack tables," I say, pointing one out to Hugh in the far left corner of the casino.

"Let's see how much we have to have to get on the table," Hugh says.

"Oh, wow. I guess you have to start with $5,000 as your minimum according to the dealer," I say with my jaw dropped.

"Let's do it."

"Are you crazy? That's too much. I'm not that good at this game to gamble that kind of money away."

"I've tried my hand at Russian Roulette before, love. It's not that much."

"Maybe to you, but that's a ton for me."

"If it feels like we're about to lose, we will walk away. I spent more than that on your bag today. I need to earn it back."

"Whatever you say, Mr. Money Bags. That would be nice if you could break even."

•••

Hugh places money on the table and waits for the dealer to start the game. My palms are sweaty and my heart is racing. Once we're ready, Hugh places half of the white chips in front of him saying he wants to put half at stake. I can't believe my eyes, and I think it's kind of a foolish move if I'm being frank. I know I'm not a gambler, and I don't have experience, but it seems like a hasty move.

"Scarlett, just relax, love. I have this under control. I promise."

"You don't know what you're doing, do you?" I say with a giggle.

"I've gambled with friends plenty of times. I've been to Vegas, and I've gambled there as well. I wouldn't risk five grand if I didn't think I could win."

"Okay, well, just play it safe. I'm nervous."

"You being nervous is like shouting when someone is driving and you think they're going to crash the car. It never helps the person."

"Okay! Okay! I get it. I'll sit over here and sip this wine."

"Good. Thank you."

I've never seen Hugh this intense. Had I known he would turn into this money maniac, I wouldn't have agreed to come. I'm not exactly liking this side of him, but I understand that gambling is risky business. I guess after this we can go back to the resort and be loving and normal towards each other. It's good for me to see this side of Hugh before getting too deep into our relationship. I'm just saying that it's good to really know someone and their triggers before getting serious. I have times where I'm not myself, and when I clam up or get bitchy, mostly when I'm really hungry. I don't think we will be spending much time at casinos in the future.

•••

I couldn't handle the pressure of watching Hugh potentially waste all of his money, so I walked away from the table and went to the bar for a drink. I don't usually get this nervous, but I guess potentially throwing thousands of dollars away scares the hell out of me.

"Can I have a shot of anything strong?" I ask the bartender, hoping he speaks English.

"Of course. Coming right up."

I throw back the shot of whiskey and make a scrunched up face because it's disgusting. I'm not much of a whiskey girl unless it's camouflaged in some lemonade or something cinnamon-flavored. I feel the burn in my chest and start to feel a pang of heat throughout my body. I ask for another. Then another. After almost four shots of whiskey, I think I'm ready to go back to the table.

"HUGH, darling, what's going on?" I say as I stumble all over him.

"What's going on, love? You smell like a frat boy," Hugh replies.

"Just had to get away to make sure I didn't ruin your game."

"You didn't ruin anything. In fact, I think you might be my good luck charm considering I'm about to win big."

"How so?"

"I'm about to have 21."

"Holy shit. Are you counting cards?"

"Be quiet! Of course I'm not. Don't say stuff like that in here," Hugh whispers loudly.

•••

The whiskey probably wasn't my best idea of the night, but I care exponentially less than I did before. The problem with that is, my voice has gone up several octaves since earlier when I did care. I don't like the seriousness this casino has caused between us. I'm so ready to just walk out of here and go to the hotel. Maybe I will. I'm over this.

"Enjoy your game," I say as I get up from the table.

"Where are you going, Scarlett?"

"Away from here."

"Don't leave," Hugh says as he gets up from the table to convince me to stay.

"I don't like this. I don't even recognize you right now."

"I'm sorry. I'm almost done. I promise."

"Okay. Whatever."

I walk away from the table, go to the front of the casino, and decide to wait for Hugh there instead of leaving for the resort. I started thinking about how I could put myself in a "Taken" situation. That movie will forever haunt me when I'm alone in a car without someone with me, especially in a foreign country. I feel let down by the evening, I hate to admit. I wanted everything about this weekend to be perfect. I guess nothing is perfect, except for this lobby. It's pretty great. I love sitting here watching all the luxury vehicles being brought to the front by the valet drivers. My buzz is wearing off, and I'm getting tired and growing impatient with Hugh.

I feel a squeeze on my shoulders from behind and hope to God that it's Hugh.

"I won."

"You won? What did you win?"

"Blackjack. I just won eight-thousand euros."

"Are you shitting me? That's crazy?!"

"I'm not shitting you. I told you I would win. I actually wasn't expecting to win, but I guess I got lucky. Please don't hate me. I know I was being serious earlier. I don't like when you're upset with me."

"I don't hate you, but I don't want to go to casinos with you ever again. I didn't enjoy watching the madness."

"I totally understand. We will cross casinos off the list of activities we enjoy together."

"Thanks. Can we go back to the resort now?"

"As long as you'll cheer up and be happy again."

"I'm trying to. I just didn't like the way you were acting towards me."

"Scarlett, baby, I'm so sorry."

"Don't baby me. You were wrong to treat me like that."

"I really am sorry. I was taking it way too seriously. You're right."

"Okay. Let's just start over."

"Deal."

# Sixteen

## Skinny Dip

I guess in every relationship you're bound to see your significant other rear their ugly head every once and a while. I never thought I would see that side of Hugh this soon into things. I imagine he's gambled before to be able to win like he just did. Something tells me that he has the proclivity to do things like gamble when he's not supposed to because he gets some kind of high when he does. My uncle who passed away used to gamble all of the time. Aunt Liz used to find him gambling on the Internet on all kinds of stuff you wouldn't even expect someone to waste their money on. It caused some real problems between the two of them. I sometimes wonder if that's the reason they didn't have children.

After we got back to the hotel, Hugh tried his best at winning me over with a nice bottle of champagne and some chocolate covered strawberries he had sent to our room. I guess he called before he met me at the front of the casino to have it waiting for us when we arrived. I can't say I'm that mad considering he was able to win his money back plus more. I still don't think it's something we will ever do again as a couple. Some things just need to be done alone. I don't drag Hugh shopping with me when I want to buy a new pair of shoes. Although, I must say, Hugh wouldn't mind shoe shopping. He seemed to enjoy picking out my Chanel bag a little too much. To say Hugh might be a little bit metro might be an understatement.

"You know, I can't apologize forever. Please come out on the balcony and enjoy this champagne and listen to the ocean. I promise never to put you through that again," says Hugh in remorseful tone.

"I guess I'm having a harder time getting over it since I've never seen you like that before," I say from the bathroom as I take off my jewelry and wash my face.

"Babe, I swear. I will not gamble anymore. Now come out here! It's our last night here."

"Okay. Give me one minute."

I decided to put on some of the lingerie that Zoe snuck into my suitcase. She told me that any time you go on a romantic getaway, the guy expects some kind of thank you. This is the "thank you" we came up with when we were packing Thursday night. I got this black, lacey number from a lingerie store in St. Germaine the other day. I wanted to wear it on Valentine's Day, but I know we will be busy with Fashion Week. Might as well wear it now while we have this alone time together. Now I wish I hadn't washed my face off because I look like a teenager wearing a grown-up outfit. I guess if I put the heels back on that I was wearing it won't be as bad.

"Oh my word! What is this scandalous looking negligee? I love it!"

"I got this for Valentine's Day, but I wanted to show you now while we're here. Also, I wanted to prove I'm over things. I'm moving on. This is not a reward though… you must behave from now on."

"Is that some kind of dirty talk… because I love it. Wow, Scarlett Hanes! You look sexy as hell."

"Thank you… now come in here and take it off of me."

"I have an idea. Why don't we put those robes on, and go down to the pool for a dip."

"It's freezing! No way!"

"There's a heated indoor pool, silly. That's what I was referring to."

"You want to go skinny dipping?"

"Yes, I actually do. I've never done it."

"You're lying. I can tell by the way you just giggled that you've done it plenty of times."

"Okay, maybe you're right, but that was ages ago and I want to do it with the woman I love."

"It's not my first rodeo either, cowboy. I have been skinny dipping and I'm good at it."

"Oh, is that right? Prove it."

"You're on."

•••

Okay, so I lied. I've never been skinny dipping in my life because the thought is terrifying. I don't want Hugh to think I haven't lived on the edge, so I lied, a little. I didn't want to lie to Hugh anymore, but this is just an innocent little lie. He'll never know if I act confidently. Truth is, I'm not excited to get into a pool at this resort with people looking on those security cameras. Watch my naked body show up on all of the French tabloids tomorrow. That would make my family proud. I know it's probably an innocent crime. Hell, I don't think it's a crime at all in France. I'm pretty sure all of France condones the topless beach situation. I'll just have to go with it when we get down there. Act like I've done it a million times. I sometimes worry that I'm not the perfect girl for Hugh – that maybe I'm not adventurous enough. Perhaps he would be better off dating someone that has lived a little longer than I have… someone with more worldly experience. Let's face it – I'm not that worldly.

We make it down the elevator in our white, terry-cloth robes holding hands and giggling. Of course, Hugh brought the bottle of champagne with us so we can get even drunker to handle this daunting little adventure. I take the bottle from his hand and chug it down. I think that might be a dead give away that I'm nervous. I don't care. I need some liquid courage right now to handle this. It was daring enough to put this lingerie on for him. I've actually never purchased lingerie in my life. Where would I put it anyways? In the sock drawer at my mom's house? I don't think so.

We try to avoid any hotel staff on our way into the indoor pool and spa area. It's hard to be quiet when I'm buzzed and laughing with Hugh about the mischief we are about to be in. Hugh grabs us a few towels from the sauna and steam room area, and we go put our stuff on the pool chair.

"Okay, let's strip," says a daring and very drunk Hugh.

"You first!"

"No, you! You're the devil who's done this a million times."

"Fine. I will. At least I have something to strip out of. You're the one with nothing on under your robe."

"Good point."

I slowly take off the black corset looking thing and the thong to match. I feel so awkward doing this considering I've never done it before. I shouldn't feel weird getting naked in front of Hugh, but it feels like I have an audience for whatever reason. This is different than any other time I've taken my clothes off in front of him. I feel like I'm at the gynecologist and I'm about to have a pelvic exam. It's that awkward. I try to be sexy while doing this, but I have no grace. I trip on my shoe and fall onto the lounge chair. Of course, Hugh laughs at me. I don't care. I just want this to be over with already. Once I'm undressed and naked as a jaybird, Hugh throws his robe on the lounge chair and jumps into the pool.

"See, it's not that bad. It feels amazing in here," Hugh says as he swims near me.

"Yes, you're right. It does feel pretty incredible in here. It's like a huge bathtub that you can move freely in. I feel liberated. It feels so empowering."

"You act like you've never done this before," Hugh says as he pulls me into him.

"Well, I have. Trust me."

"Okay, well, I'm glad we're here together. This has been a fun weekend with you, Ms. Hanes."

"It has. Thank you for bringing me, Mr. Hamilton."

We both turn around at the sound of the door slamming and freak out wondering whom it could be. This was my hunch. I was afraid we would get caught, kicked out of the hotel, and be forced to leave.

"Sortez! Sortez!" yells the French man who apparently works in the hotel.

We try our best to get out of the pool by covering ourselves and grabbing the towels and all of our belongings. The man stood there watching us like a pervert. I guess if he hadn't, we would have stayed in a little longer. I couldn't believe he just waited there until we were out of the pool. I'm starting to realize why I have yet to skinny dip in my twenty-three years on this earth. There are low-reward, high-risk situations, and this is one of those situations. I feel kind of humiliated. I guess I just wanted the first time we went skinny dipping together to be a little bit more *romantic*. Everything tonight has turned to shit. I wish we could just start our night over completely. Oh well, I guess nothing can be perfect. Life isn't always what you expect it to be. I'm starting to learn that since I've been abroad these last few weeks.

# Seventeen

## Waxing-Poetic

Do you ever have days where you just sit at your desk and wonder where you are going with your life? Today has been one of those days. After we got back from Monaco, time slowed down and things were put into perspective. I really love Hugh, I do. I just don't know if I can picture getting engaged any time soon. Since I first laid eyes on Hugh, I knew I could see myself having a future with him. Everything has been kittens and rainbows for the most part. I just wonder if those rainbows were clouding my judgment a bit. How do you ever really and truly know somebody? I guess I don't know all of Hugh's faults. Hell, if he knew mine, he probably wouldn't be with me. I need to take into consideration that nobody is perfect. I must try and learn every facet of Hugh before I commit to a lifelong journey down the aisle. I want to think he has very few flaws, but there is still so much that I don't know. I don't even really know what his house looked like that he grew up in as a kid or where he went to grade school. I don't know what his mom's middle name is or where she's from. Those are all little things that I feel like I should know before I get married to him. Perhaps we just need to take a trip to Australia this summer. Although, I'm not sure that I want to go in the summer because it's their winter when it's our summer. So confusing. I guess it would be nice to go in the wintertime.

Part of me knows I'm feeling antsy because I'm anxious about Addison and Claire coming to visit. Then, there's my birthday, Valentine's Day, and Fashion Week all within ten days. All of those things are quickly approaching and I didn't realize how fast my life was moving until today when I was working on some articles in preparation for the upcoming events. I can't believe we've already been in France for nearly six weeks. I feel like time is flying by faster here than it does back in New York. I guess I'm enjoying the work here and the atmosphere, too. I think I'm enjoying the croissants and pastries more than I anticipated considering my pants are feeling a lot more snug than they did when I got here. I feel like good food will always be my downfall. I don't have much willpower when it comes to the smell of warm, buttery croissants and espresso from a block away. Everyone has assured me I can lose the weight but I can't experience this the way I am now. I'm just going to take their advice and indulge while I still can.

I heard from my mom this morning, and I feel like she's hiding something from me for some reason. It could be all the dubiety in my life right now, but she never just calls me out of the blue, especially not at six in the morning her time. She said she was calling to tell me she loved me so much and she misses me. She didn't mention the health of either of my grandparents, what my dad or sister were up to, or even her for that matter. She just called to let me know she was thinking of me. She knows how I am constantly eager for updates on my grandparents, yet she won't give them to me. She thinks she's protecting me by not telling me information. My mom, being in politics, sometimes has the proclivity to spin things and hide the truth.

As I sit here, looking out at the magical streets of Paris, I wonder what my family is doing back home. I know I need to be focusing on my writing, but I can't. When we got back from Monaco, I didn't see Hugh for three days. I just needed some space. I loved the good aspects of our trip, but there's just something so indistinct that I can't put my finger on about our relationship. It crosses my mind quite often that Hugh might be the man I spend the rest of my life with, but I just don't know. All I really want to do is have fun with my best friend and her sister for the next ten days and focus on work.

Tonight, everyone from *Hearst* is meeting for dinner to discuss plans for Fashion Week and where we will be during each event. I know I'll see Hugh there, and we'll be forced to talk. Unfortunately, I still picture him at that blackjack table, so dogmatic, as if he was inoculated from losing. He had the craziest disposition that night – something I don't ever wish to experience in the future. I know it shouldn't bother me so much, but I'm concerned he will get hurt one day if he gets in gambling trouble. I know he wants to see me because he's been blowing up my phone these past couple of days. He's been busy working with the models for the shows and taking headshots for all the major labels. I can't say I love that he spends most of his days with gorgeous women who have legs that come up to my boobs and are flawless in every way. I guess it's the nature of working as a photographer for a major magazine. I'm not even the insecure or jealous type. I just don't really like it right now with the way I feel.

With the way I felt after speaking to my mom, I decide to take a break from *taking a break* and call my grandfather. I know he will make me feel better and tell me what's *really* going on back home. I really miss home right now and would do just about anything to hug his neck and sit on their porch swing. I would love to take a stroll to Battery Park and smell the brackish air and look at my favorite Spanish moss trees blowing in the wind. Also, most people hate the smell of plough mud, but until you live in Charleston, you won't understand. It's something you only experience in the low country. Grandfather knows everything about the history of the houses on Broad Street and all the other famous streets downtown. We used to walk along the cobblestone sidewalk and listen to him talk of the aristocratic people that lived in the houses before he even got there. I guess he's been on a carriage tour a time or two. I never minded listening to the stories over and over. There's something to be said about a relationship as strong as we have. The bond my grandfather and I have is pretty incredible, and I wouldn't trade it for anything. Thankfully, Savannah was able to teach him how to video chat on his tablet so we can see each other while I'm here.

I call his number and wait for him to pop up on the screen, but it was my grandmother instead.

"Scarlett, darling! How are you?"

This is the first time I've seen her without hair. I try my best to hold back my tears, but they come streaming out.

"Oh my gosh. It's so good to see you. I love that headscarf! Did you get that from Gwynn's? I heard they remodeled the entire store. I can't wait to go with you when I get back."

"I know it's hard to see me like this, but I'm doing okay. I feel a lot stronger than I look. I promise."

"You look fabulous, grandmother. I can't believe it. Where's grandfather? I was hoping to say hello."

"Oh, I'm sorry, honey. He's actually taking a quick nap right now. With me up at all the hours of the night, he's been running around and helping with the nurses and he's exhausted. He's been getting himself quite worked up since I've been ill. We will have to arrange a better time to talk soon. Selfishly, I'm glad I get to talk to you instead."

"Oh, that's too bad. Please let him know I called. I'm worried about you two. I worry so much about your health and how you're holding up."

"Please, honey, don't worry about us. We want you to take every moment you're over there and soak it in. You're young, and beautiful, and *so* smart. Just enjoy yourself! No need for worrying."

"Alright. Thank you for your reassurance. I would like to think if something were wrong, you would tell me. Mom called me this morning, and it was a very cryptic conversation. It had me feeling uneasy. That's why I called."

"We are so excited to see you when you come back home. Don't worry about us, darling. How is that hot boyfriend of yours?"

I don't understand why she feels the need to change the subject when clearly I'm concerned. This is all so bizarre to me. Grandfather has never been one to "nap" because he always said he can sleep when he dies. I'm starting to feel annoyed that everyone thinks they have to treat me with kid gloves now that I live in a foreign country.

"I *always* worry. I love you guys more than anything. Hugh is doing fine. He took me to Monaco for a weekend holiday. That's what he calls a vacation."

"Your mother told me about your holiday. How romantic. Do you think you two will be making plans for marriage any time soon? You know how I feel about you two living together and going off like that."

"Yes, I know how you feel. Thank you for loving me despite our choices. You know, I don't know. I thought so until this past weekend, actually. Something tells me I'm too young or that he might not be the one for me."

"What makes you think something so crazy? You two have *real* chemistry. You look amazing together, and you're in love. I might not approve of the whole living situation, but I can get past my ancient ways. What happened between you two?"

"Let's just say, loving him is a *gamble*. I really care deeply about him. I've never allowed myself to be this vulnerable with anybody."

"It sounds like you are just tired. I wouldn't write the script, Scar. You two love each other and you are on the trip of a lifetime in Paris. Take every moment of the day to carpe diem. You are only this young and not tied down by life for a short time. Soon, I hope, you'll have a family of your own so you can tell them the wonderful memories you're creating. You'll look back and regret it if you don't give it a chance."

"I know. You're right. You're so wise. I guess with me turning a year older in a couple of days I'm just waxing poetic. I don't usually reflect this much on my actions or my future. I just want to make the next year something to remember. You know what I mean, right?"

"Of course, my beautiful grand baby! I can remember the first time I ever held you in my arms. You were so tiny. Your cheeks were so vibrant and red. You looked up at me and I fell in love immediately."

It's hard for me not to cry right now. I see my grandmother speaking so highly of me and slow tears running down her face. I miss her so much. I worry I'm going to lose her before I get the chance to give her a proper goodbye.

"You're making me sad! I don't like getting older. I want to be a kid again."

"Scarlett, life is a privilege that not everyone is given, unfortunately. Life can be taken from us so quickly. Don't ever take for granted the aging process, just the wrinkles, because God knows they aren't fair."

"I'm sorry. I shouldn't say those kinds of things to you, especially not in your situation. I love my life. I love you. I have to go finish some work before a dinner I'm attending tonight. I promise I will call again soon. After Fashion Week."

"It's alright, darling. I love you *very* much. Please know that. Keep us in your prayers. You're never far away from me. You're right in my heart."

"As are you. Love you so much."

Something isn't right. I just feel like something is *totally* wrong. I don't like when people keep things from me, especially my *family*, the people I trust most. I'm glad this day is almost over. I'm ready to see Hugh tonight and give him a big hug and kiss. If my grandmother is right, and we really do have the kind of chemistry that most could only dream of, we need to figure this out. I need to see him and make things right. I need Hugh right now more than ever. He's the only one here that I truly have to lean on before Addison and Claire arrive on Wednesday. He's the only one who really knows what's going on in my life.

# Eighteen
## City of Love

The conversation I had with my grandmother had me re-evaluate my situation and what I really want with my life. I thought that I could go on without Hugh, but I was wrong. Sometimes, I think it takes situations like this to really put life into perspective. When I saw him at the event last night, it hit me that I couldn't imagine him with anyone else. Not that I would be jealous – I just can't picture him with anyone but me. I tried to imagine what my life would be like without Hugh. I realized that my life was extremely lame before he came into my life. Not to mention, I would be homeless when I returned to New York City if we broke up.

That's the other thing. I was starting to realize that maybe I don't want to be in the city anymore. Maybe I want to be close to my family with all that's going on back home. I'm sure that I could get a job just about anywhere now that I have *Hearst Magazines* on my resume. It would be hard to leave such an amazing company. I wonder if Hugh would ever consider leaving Hearst to move to Charleston with me. He has said how much he adores Charleston. I don't want to write it in the sand just yet. I just want to figure out what I want. Typical woman. Never knowing what she truly wants until it's gone.

When we left the dinner, Hugh and I went on a walk by the Eiffel Tower. He said he wanted to talk to me and spend some time with me before Valentine's Day tomorrow. We decided not to do anything major since we already went to Monaco, and Fashion Week is happening in literally a minute. Courtney has been sending me tons of projects to work on in preparation for the big event, too. I still haven't quite wrapped my head around the fact that I was chosen to come to Paris. I'm sure when I'm older, I will look back on this and wonder how it flew by so fast and how I took this wonderful time in my life for granted. Who doesn't take these types of things for granted at this age?

I can't stop thinking about everything I want to show the girls when they arrive in a couple of days. There are still many things I myself haven't seen that I'd like to explore. Unfortunately, I'll only have a few days to really spend with Addison and Claire before I have to buckle down and prepare my segments for next week. Courtney wants me to interview five designers and ten models that are in the show. I've been trying to pick new designers and new models so that I'll have a better chance of getting their attention. I know if I even try to interview Gigi Hadid, I'd probably be laughed out of the room. I'm nobody, and at Paris Fashion Week, she's everything.

As we walk by the most beautiful landmark in the world, all I can think about is the upcoming events in my life. I have a habit of planning out my future, in long-term scenarios, and getting totally lost in space.

"Scarlett, what are you thinking about? You are totally out of it!" Hugh asks curiously.

"I'm sorry, love. I can't stop thinking about everything in our lives right now. With Valentine's Day being tomorrow, I wonder how I got so lucky to be here with you. I'm also a bit nervous about the Webster sisters coming with all we have going on at work."

"We are lucky to be here. I'm so happy to be in love with you in the most romantic city on Earth. Don't stress about work. You're going to do great. If you need any help getting those interviews, you know I have some connections."

"I know you do. I didn't want to have to rely on you for help, but in order to keep from pulling out my hair; I might need you to introduce me. Nobody says 'NO' to Hugh Hamilton."

"Of course. I will try and make sure you are taken care of when everything is chaotic. Just remember to breathe. And to sneak some time in for me so that I don't pull my hair out!"

This is something I've always said about Hugh – he always knows the perfect thing to say to calm me down. He's always been there for me when I need reassurance and guidance at work. I can't imagine my life without him even though he's only been in my life for such a short time. Hugh being older and wiser helps when I'm in new situations like Paris Fashion Week. He's worked Fashion Week in New York City and Paris, several times, to know what to expect. I feel like a fish out of water – a really little fish in a huge ocean of big fish.

"Let's go get a crepe and call it a night," says Hugh as he grabs my hand to go towards the food truck.

"I can't believe I'm eating chocolate crepes the week before Fashion Week. The models probably haven't had anything but water sandwiches since September."

"Good thing you have great genes and you can afford to eat a crepe or twelve. You look incredible. Also, all this walking you've been doing in the city has made you look extra thin."

"Why are you being so sweet?!"

"I'm being honest! You look great, Scarlett. Stop worrying. It's Valentine's Day in two hours. Maybe we should head back to our flat and start the day off right."

"Fair enough," I say back with a smirk.

Luckily, we don't live very far from the Eiffel Tower so we can just walk back since it's not a cold night tonight. It's late, but not that cold. Maybe I'm just getting used to this balmy air NYC prepared me for. I'm ready to curl into bed with Hugh and fall asleep in his arms. This is the first Valentine's Day since high school that I've had a boyfriend. It feels nice to be loved on the one day you should feel loved the most.

# Nineteen

## BON-jour!

I can't believe Valentine's Day ended so quickly! Between work, going home to get ready for dinner with Hugh, then dinner with Hugh… the day went by so fast. I wish it were Valentine's Day more often. Hugh made me feel really special yesterday. He makes me feel really special everyday, but yesterday was something else. Hugh's idea of a casual dinner was eating at the Eiffel Tower. Not at the Eiffel Tower, but *inside* the tower. It was scary being up so high, but probably one of the best meals I ever had. He had rose petals all over the table and the floor with a little candle in the middle to set the mood. I'm sure he paid so much extra to have all the little added perks. We didn't do gifts, because I really don't know what to get the man who has everything, but we did give each other really sweet cards. He said some romantic things I could never compete with, but I did okay with mine as well.

Today is the day I get to be reunited with my best friend in the whole wide world. I haven't seen Addison since Christmas when we ran into each other at the airport. Well, we saw each other over break to exchange gifts, but not for very long. I see Claire in the city here and there, but we don't spend much time together. She invited Claire so that when they leave Paris, she'll have someone with her to explore the other countries. I cleaned my flat from top to bottom, and I was able to get Zoe to stay with Trey for the next few nights so they can stay with me. It's nice that she is willing to do that, but Zoe doesn't mind at all. I had no idea when I was paired with Zoe that we'd actually be compatible roommates and friends. I tried to buy some American snacks and toiletries for the girls' visit so they'd feel like they were at home. I know that seems odd to buy American goodies since they just came from there, but the food is sometimes daunting to try and you just need a little normalcy. I made sure to stock up on good wine and champagne. You can get alcohol here cheaper than water or juice. Might as well get on the wine train while I have my friends in town.

Since I enjoyed the bike tour so much during the day, I planned a night tour to try out with the girls for tomorrow evening. I figured they would be tired tonight since they just got here, and we could do something low-key and catch up since it's been so long. Apparently, Addison has a boyfriend she's been dating since she started school last year. I wanted to hear all the crazy details in person since Addison is such an animated person. I do know his name is Ford, and he's a third-year law student. She's always liked older guys, but never really settled down with anyone for this long. Addison said before she went to Georgetown that she wouldn't settle down with anyone until she was out of school. That didn't exactly go as planned, but if anyone knows that love can't be planned, it's me. Sometimes it's the right place and the right time that make things happen the way they're supposed to. Hopefully, we will both get married and have kids around the same time so we can raise them together. We always said that would be a fairytale, as cliché as that sounds.

My flip phone is ringing from the bathroom where I left it while I was getting ready for their arrival.

"Oh my gosh! Are you guys here? Where are you?"

"I CAN'T BELIVE WE MADE IT! OH MY GOD! This place is incredible! We are just now getting off the train at the REN Station, and we are getting on the metro to come to your flat," Addison loudly exclaims.

"I can't wait to see you two! I'm seriously so excited. If you need anything, don't hesitate to call or text me. I'm so glad you bought that international plan for your phone!"

"See you in about thirty minutes… if we don't get lost."

I can't believe they are finally here. I feel like I have a piece of home coming to see me. I feel whole, like my family is coming. Who am I kidding? They *are* family. I'm so happy I get to see them and spend quality time before the shows gear up next week. I wish my mom and sister could have made it, but Savannah has a new job that she's working all through her spring break, and my mom has so much going on since Trump was elected last fall. I don't get into politics much, but I can say this will be an interesting four years.

I hear the buzzer chime at the door signaling me to let the girls in. I check my hair in the mirror, as if they give a damn what I look like, and run downstairs at lightning speed.

"BON-jour, Scarlett Hanes!" says Addison in her very southern accent. It's funny how she pronounces that word.

"Oh. My. God. I can't believe you are finally here!"

Addison throws her stuff on the ground and nearly picks me up to hug me. I hug Claire and help them with their stuff up the stairs to my loft. There are so many things I want to talk about with them, but I can't find the words. I'm just too excited to even know where to start. It's funny how you can catch up instantly with good friends, as if you haven't spent one day apart. I want to know everything.

"This is so cute! I love your apartment, Scarlett," Claire says as she's admiring Zoe's side of the room.

"That's my roommate's side. She's way more eclectic than I am. I think you two will get along. She's been nice enough to stay with her boyfriend so you girls will have a bed to sleep on. It's nice we don't have twin beds. Hopefully you can squeeze in that full-size bed. It might be a bit like Polly Pocket, but it's better than the floor I suppose."

"No, this is perfect. We are so thankful you are allowing us to hone in on your living space like this," Claire says.

"Yeah, thanks, Scarlett. You're the best!" Addison chimes in.

"I wouldn't have it any other way. If you were in a hotel, I'd want to stay with you! I feel lucky you want to stay with me. The more time together, the better."

"Where's Hugh? I wanted to say hello at some point this week," Addison asks.

"You'll see him at dinner tonight. He's agreed to chaperone us to some cool Japanese fusion restaurant near the Louvre."

"That sounds perfect. I love Japanese food," Addison says with excitement.

"I know you do, honey. That's why I suggested Hugh find us something fun and unique. I'm sure you're hungry now."

"I'm always hungry, Scarlett. You know this," Addison says while looking at the snacks over my mini fridge.

"Help yourself to some snacks."

"Thanks! Is it too early to start drinking?"

"It's Paris. It's never too early to start drinking!"

We open a bottle of champagne to toast the night and the next few days we have together. We finished the bottle in less than twenty minutes, so it's probably a good thing I bought several. I haven't really had much to drink since being here unless I was out to dinner with Hugh. But still, I hardly ever get the chance to really explore Paris the way I want to. Of course, Hugh has been great, but it's different with your girlfriends. It's very different; very,

"Sex and the City" if you know what I mean.

We take turns getting showered and beautiful for dinner tonight. I can't wait to take them out in the city to see Paris lit up at night. It's my favorite time of day here. Everything is shining and beautiful. People never slow down at night in Paris. It feels similar to New York, but I never know what anyone is saying. I'm starting to get used to being here... as it's getting closer time to me leaving. I think everything in life happens like that, unfortunately.

# Twenty
## Red, Red, Whine

"Is this going to be difficult for those who are out of shape? I don't bike on a regular basis. I get blisters walking from campus to my car," whines Addison as we prepare for our bike tour.

"You clearly never lived in New York City, my adorable sister."

This was surprising for me to hear from Claire. I would have thought Addison, being the jock, would have been all for this activity. Clearly, grad school has taken a toll on her capability to jump outside her comfort zone. "Walking and riding bikes is a way of life where we live!"

"Trust me. If I can do this, anyone can. Hugh and I took a guy from work that had never even been on a bicycle. Top that!" I say, laughing to the girls.

"Yeah, you girls will do just fine," Hugh, says, trying to be apart of the "girls night out" situation.

I would normally think it's humorous, but they have a point. These bike tours usually consist of over twenty miles of riding around Paris. Not to mention, we walked *a lot* today when we went shopping. I've never been the girl with skinny thighs until living the city life. I wish I could say that about the rest of my body. Why won't my body just be skinny all over? I don't want to be "skinny," per-say; I just want to be able to wear my clothes and not look like Jabba the Hut. I'm so envious of all the long-legged Parisian girls. I must say, though, Hugh has never made one snide comment about my body type, or any female's, for that matter. I have so much respect for a man that does not make snide comments about a woman's looks. Men who put women down are the scum of the Earth.

Hugh arranged for an Uber to pick us up at our flat to take us to Fat Tire Bike Tours by the Eiffel Tower. This particular tour is unique from the others because it's at night and you get to take a boat cruise across the Seine. The instructor will bring red wine for everyone to enjoy while we are on the boat. In America, that might earn you a "B.U.I," also known as, "biking under the influence." Quite possibly the dumbest thing I ever heard. I see people in Charleston getting these on King Street, every weekend, outside Wet Willies. People just ride their bikes to get frozen cocktails and think they can ride home without the men in blue coming after them. My grandfather usually refers to them as "liquor-cycles" which is pretty humorous coming from him.

However, we are in Paris, and anything goes in Europe it seems. I see teenagers drinking beers at three in the afternoon most days. It's actually sad to see kids getting into that kind of trouble at such a young age. When I was their age, I was playing with my American Girl Dolls.

•••

The tour starts in nearly fifteen minutes and we are still waiting for our Uber. If I haven't mentioned this yet, Europeans are the original inventors of the term, "fashionably late." I've never waited for food longer in my life than at a French restaurant. Americans like things hot, fast, and clean. These restaurants act like they are doing you the biggest favor serving you, too. I think not tipping in Europe is their punishment for poor service. I would tip if it would speed up the process. Waiting until seven in the evening to open for dinner is just a crazy notion in my mind. I don't know why they don't accept tips, but I have a feeling it has something to do with the high price of goods here.

Speaking of goods, the group decided we should bring wine in our purse as a "pre-game" to our outing. When I say group, I mean me. I thought it would be fun to push the envelope for once. Addison is usually the one pushing the envelope in these situations, as you already know. I'm seeing a different side of her in Paris. I'm wondering if grad school has been a humbling experience for her. Maybe she's realized that becoming an attorney is quite the daunting process.

We start to pass the bottle around to drink from, and I'm thinking to myself, "Herpes is for life, you know," but I imagine nobody here has herpes. I just don't find drinking after somebody something I enjoy doing. I always worry that I'll get sick and then feel like complete crap the rest of the week-end. Whenever I'm tipsy, I usually don't give a damn. This is one of those times. I'm sure that my parents would advise against me riding a bicycle in a foreign country after too many drinks, but they aren't here are they?

"Let's play never have I ever," Claire says after chugging half the bottle.

"What's that?" Hugh asks curiously.

"I say something I've never done, and if you have done it, you drink!" Claire says.

"I see," Hugh says.

"We used to play it in college all the time. Don't you remember, Addison?" I ask hoping she doesn't bring up the time we played and I ended up having to chug a Smirnoff Ice and recite the fifty states song.

"Oh, yes, I remember quite well," Addison laughs, and we both know why.

"Well, I'll start," Claire, says.

I'm wondering what Claire is going to say. For quite some time, I have thought that Claire had a crush on Hugh. I don't know what it is about her, but I feel like she wants to be around him. Every single time we see her, she tries laughing at things he says or she makes comments that make me feel like she's attracted to him. Before she arrived in Paris, I had a strange premonition that she would flirt with my boyfriend when she got here.

"Never have I ever kissed someone from another country," Claire says as she sits on the curb as we wait for our driver.

WOW, what are her intentions by saying that? To get me drunk or to signal to Hugh that she wants to kiss him? It's hard to tell. I'm going to try not to let that get to me. I snatch the bottle from her and drink for nearly a minute. The taste of this bitter wine is killing my throat, but I don't care. I'm irritated. It seems like girls can't ever truly get along. I think the reason I get along so well with Addison is because she's basically a guy.

Luckily, as I finish chugging the merlot, our driver pulls to the curb. I was glad that game didn't have a very long run considering the next thing I was going to say was, "Never have I ever slapped a girl square in the face!"

# Twenty-One
## I'm so Ty-red

We arrive at Fat Tire Bike Tours and I sign everyone in with our reservation. Hugh and the Webster sisters went and sat at a table with two other girls. They were both beautiful girls, but one of them stood out to me in particular. I noticed her from somewhere, but I couldn't put my finger on it. After signing in, I walk to the table to join everybody. The girls they are sitting with introduce themselves to me.

"Hi, my name is Isabella and this is my sister, Dani," she says, extending her hand.

It was strange that she wanted to shake my hand instead of kissing my cheeks. I could tell she wasn't from France. Not to mention, she had a strong accent that was distinctly something from Brazil or Portugal. I couldn't figure it out. Isabella was the beautiful girl I recognized from somewhere. I ask her what they are doing in Paris, and she said she is here for an ambassador event from Miss Universe. Then, it clicked! Miss Universe Brazil! It was her! She didn't win the competition, but she was runner-up in 2012. I've always watched the Miss Universe pageants with my mom and sister growing up. I was shocked at Isabella's beauty to be honest. She was even prettier in person than she was on TV.

"I was wondering where I knew you from! Wow. That's so amazing," I say in awe of her long shiny hair and beautiful teeth.

"I remember you now," Hugh says as he chimed in the conversation. "I was at Miss Universe in 2013, and I think I remember seeing you there."

"Why were you at Miss Universe?" I ask with both eyebrows raised.

"I was dating one of the photographers for the competition at the time. Very short lived-relationship," he says, hoping to change the subject. Of course, now, I'm curious what happened between them. I probably shouldn't dwell on it since they aren't together now, obviously.

Isabella and Dani became quick friends with our group. They were both so fun and easy to talk to. Dani is a veterinarian in Brazil, and she is married with two small children. Isabella is trying to get back in to the Miss Universe competition in some capacity. They became so comfortable with our group that we end up sharing the other bottle of wine from Addison's purse. One of the tour guides gave us some cups since we were waiting for our guide to be ready. Ironically, our tour guide is Australian like Hugh. They aren't from the same part of Australia, but Hugh has been there many times.

We met outside to go on our tour, and we got into the group with Isabella and Dani. I could tell that we would be fast friends with them and the night would be exciting.

Two hours later…

"Teacher! You give me more wine, please! Isabella insists to Paul, our tour guide for the night.

You could tell they were completely smitten with each other. Paul was a model back in his prime, but he's in France studying law and working as a tour guide part-time. He and Isabella both have the model-body in common. I must say, though, Paul is not in model shape like Isabella. I saw his Calvin Klein modeling photos from his phone, and he was once in tip-top shape. I was impressed! I couldn't get over how funny it was to hear Isabella refer to Paul as "teacher" all night. She kept asking me what to call him, and I kept telling her to call him Paul. She thought it was more fun to refer to him as "teacher" since he was our instructor.

At this point, we were all on the boat cruise on the Seine. It literally looks like a school bus on top of a boat. Not to mention, the weather is frigid since it's the middle of winter. The only thing keeping me warm, besides my coat and Hugh, is my wine coat. Literally, the wine buzz is keeping me warm to tolerate these artic wind gusts. Paul was telling us that he and his friends make hot-muddled wine and it's really good this time of year. I'd never heard of such a thing, but I'm sure it's pretty good.

We were all pretty inebriated at this point of the tour, and none of us felt like getting back on our bikes to ride three miles back to the bike tour place. I really don't want to ride anymore because I know it will kill my buzz and make me even colder. I suck it up, with the rest of the group, and we ride into the city to return our bikes. As we ride over the Lock Bridge, the Eiffel Tower starts to light up and sparkle like it does every night around this time. I will seriously never get tired of looking at this magnificent site. Every time I see it, I realize how blessed I am to be here and the opportunity only comes once in a lifetime. Not to mention, I will be leaving here pretty soon.

"Teacher, where can we get food and drink?" Isabella asks, slurring her broken English.

"There's a great Irish pub only a few minutes away that I go to on the weekends. They serve food late at night," Paul says to Isabella.

I look at my group and ask them if they would be interested in continuing this party with these people. We didn't have other plans, and we are not the type to go to a club to party. So, we decide to go with them to the Irish pub. How much trouble could we possibly get into?

You walk in this "pub", as they refer to it in Paris, and it's dimly lit, smells like beer that's been spilled all over the floor, and it's really hot. I can't complain about the warmth in here considering I can't even type on my cell phone due to extreme numbness. The smell of this place reminds me of a frat house. It's a small, dark bar with a ton of people crowded together. It had a thin layer of smog from the people smoking in the back. Smoking indoors is acceptable in France for whatever reason. All I want to do is eat a huge plate of cheese fries, but explaining that order to the French server is going to be a difficult task.

Paul knows the bartender because he said he sleeps with her on occasion. Super casual, no big deal. This girl looks much older than Paul with her crow's feet and run down look. She's not unattractive. In fact, she's quite the looker despite her rough-around-the-edges look. I'm sure she would look better if she wasn't run down. She just needs a little rest and a mini-makeover. I'm sure Paul saw her looking decent at some point and decided to pounce. He was all over Isabella from the minute they met. She's a different story, though. She's literally a Brazilian model with long legs and beautiful features. I'm wondering how this redheaded bartender would feel if she knew Paul had the hots for Isabella? Probably wouldn't have given us the VIP table in the back had she known. Then again, some women like that kind of thing. The phrase "ménage a trois" is French after all.

The entire night, we sit in this crowded bar, dance, and take a ton of shots. Of course, Claire elected to sit *right* next to Hugh. I'm really trying not to make a thing of this, but it's driving me nuts. Why couldn't she sit next to Dani or Addison? I wonder if she's just trying to be friendly. It's hard for me to trust women. I just don't understand why she'd go after my boyfriend. Unless she's just doing it because she likes him and knows she can't have him. Maybe being near him is good enough for her. Since Claire is only here temporarily, I'll just keep my mouth shut for Addison's sake. I wouldn't want to ruin my friendship over a suspicion. Tonight was really fun, and the bar was more than I expected it to be. I felt like I was on an episode of "Cheers" with the people who clearly frequent this pub on a weekly basis. It was fun and felt like home. There were two men sitting in their corner, drinking and dancing to this Elvis song, and everyone was watching. They said they had come to this Irish pub every Friday night for the past ten years! See why I said it's like the show, "Cheers?"

We had a great time despite Claire trying to cozy up to Hugh all night.

It was nearly three in the morning and we all decided it was probably time to go home. Isabella and Dani hopped in the cab with us since they were staying in St. Germaine near our flat. We got in the mini-van and Dani sat in the front seat. Isabella is in the backseat talking in her drunken, broken English saying things I barely understand. Dani is in the front saying she doesn't feel well. We began to beg the driver to pull over so she could get some fresh air, or puke, but she said she was fine.

"I fine, I fine, no worry." Dani pleads.

"If you puke in this cab, it's going to cost you. Literally, cost you. Don't do it, Dani." I instruct from the back of the cramped van.

Hugh chimed in to reiterate that she should have him pull over if she's going to get sick because it cost upwards of 300 euro if she makes a mess. We drive a few more minutes and everything is fine, and you hear Dani in the front making a funny sound.

*Boom.*

She pukes all over her Hermes scarf she bought from the Galleria today.

The driver is so furious that he pulls over onto the sidewalk and makes her get out. He walks around to the door to see if she got any puke on his seat, while yelling in French, demanding she needs to pay.

"No, it's fine. I clean." Dani says to the driver. She proceeds to clean the puke up with her Hermes scarf. I can't even watch this happen.

I'm already disgusted by the smell of this hot van we're cramped into. Isabella in the backseat saying, "I feel like I'm on movie with the drunk people on the roof." We are all looking at each other trying to decipher what she's saying to us.

"What are you talking about, Isabella?" I ask.

"You know – the movie. It's called *Very Bad Night* I think."

"What the hell are you talking about?" Claire asks Isabella.

"The fat man with the tiger in the bathroom and the baby who wear sunglasses!" Isabella tries to explain.

"I think she's referring to *The Hangover*," I say.

"Yes! That one. That funny movie where they go crazy in Vegas!" Isabella laughs. "I'm so ty-red," she whines.

"You're what?" Hugh asks.

"I need sleep."

"Tired?"

"Yes. *Ty-red.*" She tries to emphasize how sleepy she is by exaggerating the "red" in "ty-red". "That's what I said," Isabella conveys.

Everybody is dying laughing at this point. Isabella is beautiful, but when she drinks she is outrageous. It's funny to see her let her hair down – metaphorically speaking, of course. She was very proper and composed when we met at the bike shop for our tour. I have a feeling she doesn't like to let people see that side of her very often.

This night has turned out to be quite the adventure. We got out of the cab since Dani decided not to pay the driver for her incidentals. It wasn't that bad, it just smelt terrible. I was glad to get out, and we only had a few blocks to walk. Even though it's super cold, I feel warm. I'm happy to be with my friends and my new crazy friends. They are going to be in town for the rest of the weekend and want to meet up with us again. I told them we have Fashion Week starting tomorrow, and maybe we can reserve some tickets for them.

After that many drinks, I prefer to sleep in a bed tonight. I let the girls have the keys to my flat, and I went home with Hugh – for more than one reason. Maybe to send a strong message.

# Twenty-Two

## Semaine des Createurs du Mode

I woke up at five in the morning, realizing this is the reason I'm here: *Paris Fashion Week*. Today is the start of the most exciting aspect of this trip to Paris. I could not sleep last night because it feels like Christmas. It's almost like all of Paris knows that it's Fashion Week because everyone is looking mighty sharp on the subways these past few days. People go all out here for the event because it brings so many celebrities into town. I wear mostly black these days, and I'm totally okay with doing so. I was told to wear a little more makeup than usual for the shows because if I don't I will feel like an ugly duckling. I have always wanted to see the Victoria's Secret models in real life because they look so flawless on TV and in magazines. They don't seem real to me. I heard Kendall Jenner is walking for them and three other major designers. I still can't believe she's modeling in this industry.

Hugh reserved a car service for us during the show so we wouldn't have to fight over cabs or Ubers. *Cosmo* wants us to walk or ride a bike to these shows, but it's freezing outside and it's supposed to rain for the next few days, too. I don't know how I'm expected to look cute for the shows if I walk and get wet from the rain. Hugh does not like to get his hair or his shoes wet. I don't blame him though – it's nasty in the streets of Paris, when it rains,

from all the littering. We have to be at the Carrousel du Louvre by eight.
Most of the major shows Hearst is hosting are in the main arena there. There
are several shows spanning all over Paris, but this is where we will be the
entire duration of Fashion Week.

I tried prepare myself by laying out my outfit last night and consulting
with my ever-so-fashionable beau, but nothing I pick out seems to be good
enough for Fashion Week. I'm going to have to settle considering the next
week or so I'll have to look "cute" even if I don't have the proper attire.
Hugh says it doesn't matter whether I look fashionable or not. He says it's all
about how I work and if I look pulled together. He says I could literally wear
the same outfit every single day of the show if I wanted and nobody would
notice or care. He's probably right, but I don't think I could do that. I was the
girl in school who wanted to wear cute outfits to impress my friends, but, of
course, I went to private school so there's only so much you can do with a
plaid skirt and white polo. That's actually how I feel right now. How can I
dress up black jeans and a black top? I guess I can wear my hair curled or
wear extra jewelry. I don't want to look like I'm trying to be a model or
anything. I just feel like you get more respect when you dress to impress.

By 7:45, our car was outside to take us to the Louvre. I can't understand
for the life of me why I'm so nervous. It could be that Courtney has assigned
me to the Versace show tonight or that I've never done this kind of thing in
my entire life. The only kind of thing I've done like this is Charleston
Fashion Week, and I go with my mom and grandmother but I've never seen
real models in the flesh. I'm hoping to meet some of them and ask them
questions about their experiences. I'm mostly writing about their clothes and
the styles of the different shows. Courtney wants me to interview at least five
different designers if I can. Hugh said he's going to try and set me up with
some that he knows personally. Hugh seems to know everybody.

"This is Paris Fashion Week?" I ask as we walk in together holding hands. "It's incredible! I can't imagine how long it took them to set this up."

"They set it up in nearly three days. It can't be up beforehand for very long because of tourists. They have a crew of over a thousand people working to make this happen," Hugh says.

"When are we going to run into people?"

"Around lunch time. The models won't get here until then for hair and make-up, but you'll probably see some recognizable people come a little earlier."

"I want to meet Diane von Furstenberg because I hear she wears wildly glamorous outfits to these events." I don't really care about her clothes, but I watched that show on E!, so I must see her in person.

"You'll most definitely see her if you're working the Versace show. She never misses it."

"Great! I also want to interview her if I can. I need an exclusive with her. I need to be the only one from the magazine talking to her."

"You want an exclusive with Diane von Furstenberg?" Hugh looks at me like I'm crazy.

"Yes! Can you help me make that happen?"

"I don't know. That could be difficult. She doesn't really like doing interviews with the magazine anymore. Trust me, I've tried."

"Well, I need to impress Courtney. I want to prove to her that I was the right choice for Paris and it wasn't in vain."

"I can try to get you an exclusive with Tom Ford. I know his photographer from working together in the past."

"Someone you dated, I presume?"

"No, smart ass. It's actually a dude. He and I are friends."

"Oh, great! I love when it's a guy and not a girl. I don't like the girl photographer friends.'

"I know how you feel, love. Trust me." Hugh laughs and pulls me close to him to kiss the side of my head. He has a way of showing the most endearing type of affection when I need it the most. The way he looks at me has me so happy. I hate that we won't get to spend very much time together during the show, but we devised a plan to meet up every other hour until we go home to check in to see if there is anyone around to introduce me to. If I don't get these interviews, I have a feeling Courtney is going to be less than impressed.

Addison and Claire are touring around the city today until the big shows tonight. I helped map out all of the subways they need to take to get to certain landmarks. They are traveling to Versailles by train and should be here by seven tonight for the show. I've been staying with Hugh because I feel like my flat is way too cramped for three females in their twenties. Talk about a disaster with the bathroom trying to get ready in the morning. I've been fortunate in my living situations in NYC and Paris not to have to share my bathroom with more than one person. Call me spoiled, but it's majorly difficult to get ready in the morning with all the straighteners and curling irons flying around and makeup scattered everywhere. Needless to say, it's been kind of cramped for us these past few days. I love having them here, but I'm sort of ready for things to go back to normal. They have a lot to see while they're in Europe, so I don't feel so bad saying that.

Today is going to be a great day! I'm very excited for the shows tonight, and I'm ready to get this done. I told Courtney I wouldn't let her down. I don't know why I said that considering I have no idea if I'll actually accomplish what she's asking, but I'll find a way. That's how it is in this industry. You make it happen because you want to be here. If I have to pink lie a little to make it happen, I will. I know I said I was over it, but sometimes you just gotta do what you gotta do.

# Twenty-Three

## Zero is NOT a Size

You know you are important when you have front row seats to all the shows. Actually, I only have front row seats to a few of them, and the rest of them I'm in the second row. Most of the A-list celebrities and fashion icons have front row privileges. Sitting in the second row is still really prestigious from what I'm told. Being with the magazine allows a lot of special access to the shows and backstage passes. I've been trying not to think about accommodating Addison and Claire considering I gave them passes and told them where to go. I need to focus on my job so I won't let Courtney or the magazine down. I'm going to show her that I belong at this magazine. She won't be able to get rid of me!

The atmosphere can only be described in one word: chaotic. Everyone has headsets on with clipboards and they're running around yelling out things to models and producers of the show. I can't say I hate the dynamic of this place. My heart feels very full as I walk around the building of Paris Fashion Week. I'm trying to find Hugh so I can see where we are, progress wise, for getting an exclusive with someone important. Every room I go in, there are people asking me for help.

"Can you get the make-up artists for the Givenchy show? I need them NOW," says the short little Asian man as I walk backstage to the room filled with tall, skinny women.

"I'm a writer for *Cosmo*. I don't think I can help you with that," I say to him.

"Honey, you aren't as busy as me." He was clearly gay. I liked his moxie. "Just help me out and I'll make sure you get to talk to whoever it is you're looking for." He said it like he was important or he was someone who knew someone. That's the kind of person I need to know in this business.

I shuffle around backstage looking and asking for the make-up artists that could be working for Givenchy tonight. It's amusing that they even need a make-up artist for this designer. Every model I see on the runway usually looks like they have no make-up on. I'm guessing it takes more effort to achieve that look than I would suspect. I call one of the girls in the make-up department from Hearst to see if she has any clue where the artist for Givenchy might be. Thankfully, she picked up when I called and gave me a location of where they could be located.

I walk to the little Asian man, who I still don't know the name of, and tell him where they are located. Apparently, they were told to be there an hour later. I tell him I'll make the call if he can give me their number. He seems pleasantly surprised that I was able to gather that information in such a short period of time.

"Who do you work for at Hearst?" he asks inquisitively.

"Courtney in the fashion segment of *Cosmo*," I reply.

"Oh, I know that chick. I will let her know you were a big help," he says with his eyebrows raised like he's doing me a huge favor.

"Thanks. That's really nice of you. Do you know the best place for me to be to get an exclusive with Diane von Furstenberg?"

"Oh, honey, she doesn't do exclusives with just anybody. I heard she's a tough one to snatch," he replies.

"That's exactly why I want an exclusive with her. To prove my place at the magazine," I say.

"She talks to the models after shows. I do know that…"

"I'm not a model. I don't know how I'm going to make that happen."

"If you can figure out a way to get on that stage, you can get your exclusive."

"Isn't that lying? If I'm working for the magazine?"

"This is a business. You do what you gotta do to make things happen." He looks at me up and down and scrunches his face a bit. "I might be able to make your wish come true."

"Are you saying…"

"Yes, I am."

"Can you actually do that?"

"I don't think you realize who you're talking to, honey. I make *every-thing* happen around here!"

"Seriously?"

"You might have just the right look. I'll have to find some platforms for you to wear, but I like your skin and hair. You look young. That's what I need."

"You promise I won't get in trouble for this?"

"No. I can't make that promise, but I do know that DVF is attending the Givenchy show and she will be backstage afterwards."

"Oh my God. I don't know what to say."

"You can thank me later. I'm not saying she will interview with you. Only reason I'm allowing this nonsense is because Kendall Jenner backed out last minute. She broke a nail, apparently."

"Wow. I'm filling in for Kendall Jenner?"

"Not really. Just need a body to walk the stage. Nobody fills in for Kendall, honey."

Chao is the little Asian man's name that has turned my night around. I need to text Addison and Claire to go to the Givenchy show at eight tonight. They are going to flip when they see me walking the runway. I can't even believe this is my life right now. I almost don't even care if I get in trouble for this. I'll say that I was helping Givenchy. This wasn't something I asked for. They asked me. They need *me*. Chao frantically takes me to the area where the models were being fitted for their outfits. He seems a little apprehensive about his decision to have me walk the runway. I have literally zero experience doing this. I could fall flat on my face like Carrie Bradshaw did when she got her chance. I'm honestly not sure I can pull this off to be completely frank. I feel like there's no time to call Hugh and explain what is happening. I text him S.O.S. and tell him to go to the Givenchy show to make sure Addison and Claire are there. He doesn't respond with much, but he says he will be there regardless. I can't believe this is happening to me.

"We need her to be ready to walk by eight," Chao instructs the others working backstage for Givenchy.

"Who is she? How do you expect her to fit into size zero?"

"She's filling in. Make it work. I don't care if you have to duct-tape her midsection and thighs so she can't breathe. Make it happen."

At this point, I knew Chao was important considering they are listening to him. I feel as if I could puke at any moment. My body is sweating and my hands are shaking. I don't know why I'm going to such lengths to get an exclusive. It seems like they need me more than I need them though. I have to keep telling myself that I didn't ask for this. They are the ones who need me. I need to step up to the plate and make sure I deliver the best walk of my life. The only time I've ever graced the runway is during Charleston Fashion Week. The last time I participated in that event, I was, indeed, a size zero. I'm pushing a size two these days. I've consumed too many baguettes and too much red wine. I don't know how they are going to turn me into a super model in the next hour.

# Twenty-Four
## Lighting – This is What You Came For

I feel like I'm watching a dream inside of a dream, "Inception" style. I finally get the plot of that movie. The music is blaring, and the lights are so hot on my face. I don't even know what they did to make my hair stand up like this, but it stays when I touch it. My eyes have never looked this blue, and my waist has never looked this small. I swear they have transformed me into a super model in one hour. I know I'll probably never look like this version of myself ever again.

I sat next to a girl named Aubrey who is only seventeen and she's been doing this for one year. She and the hair stylist were trying to talk me off of a ledge while we were getting ready. I couldn't explain my fear for what I was about to do. I'm standing in the line of models waiting to go on stage. I'm wearing a vibrant red, backless jumpsuit with bellbottom legs, and eight-inch, gold platform heels. No joke. I've never worn shoes this tall in my life. They're heavy, and I can't figure out how I'm going to walk in them down the runway without peeing in my pants. I feel like I'm walking into cement, or quick sand when I move. I'm so nervous! My heart is about to explode. I try to think of what my grandmother says quite often, "I'd rather look good than feel good," and tonight I will live by just that. I can't explain how quickly they pulled me together. I had one girl filing my nails while the other was contouring my face and someone else tweezing my eyebrows. I feel like Sandra Bullock from "Miss Congeniality" when they give her the full-blown makeover. Surprisingly, they did not have to tape me down or suck me into Spanx to fit into this outfit.

I keep thinking to myself how I would kill to have my family here to watch this. I'm hoping the show will be filmed, and all over social media, so all the bitches back home who wouldn't let me into their cliques will drop their jaws to the floor. I have never felt this cool in my entire life. I thought it was cool to work for *Cosmopolitan*. This is way cooler. I can't stop saying cool. What is wrong with me? Anyway, I'm in shock I have made it this far in my life. I'm in shock that these are the thoughts that are running through my mind instead of thinking about how I'm going to walk without falling. This jumpsuit is longer than I would like and I'm afraid to trip over the fabric. Just as I'm about to go walk, Chao rounds the corner to tell me good luck.

"Just pretend like these people are your friends instead of extremely famous celebrities!"

"That doesn't help. Any other advice you can give me? I'm so nervous."

"Just breathe. If you need to walk slower, walk slower. I saw something in you when I met you, Scarlett Hanes. You can do this. I need you to do this. My ass is on the line for letting you walk."

"I won't let you down. Literally."

I start walking toward the front of the line and my heart sank. I feel like I'm literally going to pass out from nerves. Here goes nothing.

I don't have time to look around to see if Hugh is here. I don't pay attention to anyone; I pretend like I'm practicing and this isn't the real thing. What would my family think? Would they be proud of me for going out on a limb to participate in this show? Would they be disappointed that I was lying and not where I was really supposed to be? I can't let these thoughts plague my mind right now. I have to be a girl-boss and rock this out like none other. I lift my chin and put a fierce glare on my face.

Okay, this isn't so bad. The lights are so bright and the crowd is pitch black. The music is good and I can walk to the beat. It's as if I'm floating down this stage and I'm not even really walking. I'm just letting these clunky platform shoes walk me toward the front of the stage. I reach the end of the runway and strike a pose. No, I did not put my hand on my hip. I did, however, see Hugh in the distance and he's stunned. I quickly make the turn to head back up the runway to backstage. This has been the longest thirty seconds of my life. I can't believe I just did that without falling flat on my face. I can't even describe to the amount of cameras in my face and photographers taking my photo.

•••

It's over.

I can breathe.

Holy shit! I did it. I can't believe I just did that. I don't even know where to go right now. I look around for Chao, but all I see are models changing into their next outfit. I finally spot Chao and he runs over to me.

"You nailed it! I can't even believe you did that with such grace," he shrieks.

"I know! I'm shocked. That was exhilarating! I can't believe how nervous I was for nothing."

"It's not for nothing. You're going to be all over the Internet."

"Oh gosh. Courtney is going to KILL me. She is going to fire me as soon as she gets wind of this."

"No, honey. Courtney is going to be stoked when you get an exclusive with Naomi Campbell."

"Naomi Campbell? Are you serious?"

"Yes, I'm serious." Chao looks at me like he wanted to hug me.

"You're the best!" I say as I hug Chao like I've known him for years.

"She does not have much time since she still has to walk for Marc Jacobs at ten."

"Okay! I have some questions I can ask her right now."

I can't even believe he made this happen. I don't know why she would take the time to talk to me when she doesn't even know me. I'm sure she knows Chao, but how could he be so important that he was able to score me an exclusive? All I know is that this is just day one of Fashion Week, and I'm starting on a really high note.

# Twenty-Five
## Exclusivity

I was able to run to the back to change into my regular outfit before meeting with Naomi for my exclusive interview. I can't seem to fix my hair since it has so much hairspray in it, but I'm guessing it doesn't matter much. It will be a topic of conversation. Getting an exclusive with a famous model like Naomi Campbell is HUGE. I still have not had the chance to check my phone or look for Hugh. I have never felt more preoccupied in my life than I do right now. I'm not thinking about anything but what just happened and how I'm about to meet Naomi. Chao instructs me to meet her backstage of Marc Jacobs so she wouldn't be late to walk for the show. I don't even know where Marc Jacobs is having his show, so I ask someone that looks important. They instruct me to go to the other side of the building and I can't miss it. I have no idea how I'm going to make it to the other side of the building in the next five minutes. I'm going to be so out of breath I won't be able to ask her my questions.

I finally make it backstage and try to locate Naomi. Every model is running around and changing outfits. I'm trying to push through a sea of people to get to her. I spot her in the far left corner getting the final touches of make-up while calmly sitting in a chair.

"Ms. Campbell! How are you? My name is Scarlett, and I'm with *Cos-*

*mopolitan.*" I let her know how and why I'm standing in front of her. I tell her that Chao sent me and as soon as I did she was all smiles.

"Hello, Scarlett! So nice to meet you. I assume by the looks of your hair and make-up that you were just walking the Givenchy show with me?"

"Yes. I was in the right place at the right time I suppose. Chao needed a model last minute. I'm definitely no model, but I was able to walk without falling."

"You're a model now, Scarlett. Once you've walked that stage, you've made it to the big leagues."

"I can't even explain to you how honored I was to be walking the runway for Givenchy. I must ask, how did you start your career as a model? What is it like being so internationally known and respected?"

"I've been modeling since I was a teenager. My British background allowed me a different approach to the world of fashion. I had no idea I would make it this far in my career. Being so well-known has its ups and downs, certainly. It's brilliant most of the time."

The interview with Naomi didn't last more than five minutes since she was forced to go on stage, but I got everything I needed to report back to *Cosmo*. I'm shocked at how down-to-earth and real Naomi is. She seems to have such a kind spirit and pure heart – someone I would like to be friends with if given the chance. I knew this fairytale of a night was about to become a reality and I would be turning into a pumpkin soon. I only have to get one exclusive per show, so I'm technically done for the night. I have enough time to find Addison and Claire and catch the end of this show.

I pull my cell phone out of my bag to see that I have twelve missed calls and twenty text messages from various people. I don't even bother to look at them since I knew I wanted to call Addison and have her and Claire join me at the show.

"Hey, did you see me?"

"Oh my gosh. You are insane! We did see you!"

"Can you guys be at the Marc Jacobs show in less than five minutes? I just interviewed Naomi Campbell backstage and she gave me a pass."

"Yes! See you there."

After hanging up with Addison, I look through my texts to see if Hugh sent me any.

"Babe, you were incredible. I don't know how you ended up on that stage, but I can't wait to show you the footage I got."

I decide to call Hugh. I can't wait to tell him all about the show and what I experienced. Words really can't describe how I'm feeling right now. Cloud nine is an understatement.

"Babe! Where are you?"

"I can't talk right now. I'm about to photograph some of the models backstage at Givenchy."

"I was just there. Dang it. I'm at Marc Jacobs now."

"I'll meet you over there once I'm done. We have some major talking to do!"

"Yes. I love you!"

"Love you more."

Addison and Claire ran towards me to hug me. They both seemed so excited for me, and Claire even seemed more giddy than usual. We wanted to talk, but the show was about to begin and nobody talks during the shows. We sit in the third row and look at each other with huge smiles the entire time. I can't explain the happiness I have right now to have just experienced what I did and to be sitting with my best friend right now. To say life is good would be obvious. I'm dying to get out of here and go enjoy some champagne and food since I'm starving. I feel like I could eat an entire pizza right now after what I just did. I don't see how models are able to contain their urge to eat all the carbs in Paris after a show. Perhaps, since I won't be modeling anymore,

I can indulge a little more than usual tonight.

# Twenty-Six
## Locked Down

After the wildest night of my life, Addison, Claire, and Hugh went with me to do something I've wanted to do since arriving in Paris. It's nearly two in the morning, but I promised the girls that I would take them to the famous Lock Bridge to add the locks I had them bring from the States. Hugh told me that they take the locks off so people can add more, but I don't care. I still want to say I've been there and done that. We went to a pizza place that only opened during Fashion Week to get some late night grub and celebrate my one and done modeling career. A lot of laughing went on, and Hugh showed me some of the photos he snapped on his camera. I can't believe how amazing I looked. I'm not bragging. I'm simply amazed they were able to transform me in such a short period of time.

"What are you going to write on your lock," Claire asks us. Hugh already had a lock back at the flat, but he would re-write his message on this one.

"You'll see," Hugh says as he turns around.

"I'm going to put A & C with the date on it and a little heart," Addison says.

We were all waiting for Hugh to turn around. At this point, he was acting a little strange. I talk with the girls and just laugh about the night, waiting nearly three minutes for Hugh to be finished with the lock I gave him.

We turn around and Hugh was on one knee. My jaw just dropped. He hands me the lock and it says, "MARRY ME!" in all caps.

"Scarlett Hanes, I had planned a wonderfully romantic night with you this weekend, but sometimes timing isn't perfect. Tonight, you told me you had the best night of your life. I thought – what better time than now to keep that going. Marry me."

I'm speechless. I look at Addison and Claire and their jaws are dropped to the floor as well. I'm smiling from ear to ear and my heart is pounding. He does not appear to have a ring with him, surprisingly. I guess this truly was a moment of spontaneity.

"YES. 100% yes! Oh my God!" I squeal as Hugh picks me up to spin me around and kiss me.

"I don't have the ring with me. It's back at my flat. I'm sorry this wasn't perfect, but I wanted it to be spontaneous."

"This is amazing!! I can't even believe this is happening right now."

"You are going to make an amazing Mrs. Hamilton."

"I love the sound of that!"

Addison and Claire just so happened to have everything on camera. They took a million pictures of us while Hugh was down on one knee. I'm so happy they were able to capture our special engagement on camera. I never imagined being engaged here in my entire life. I seriously feel like tonight was better than any fairytale I have ever seen. It's like I was watching my own fairytale from the outside. I can't even explain myself right now!

"How were you able to ask for my hand in marriage so quickly? What did my dad say when you asked?"

"I asked your dad back at Christmas. I knew then that I wanted to spend the rest of my life with you."

"Even after everything that happened? You still wanted to?"

"Yes, of course."

"Does my entire family know you had this planned for months? And they've kept a secret for that long?!"

"I only told your dad and Frank. It seemed appropriate that they know since they're the most important men in your life besides me."

"I can't believe they didn't tell me!"

"They don't know we're engaged considering they were going to be here on Saturday to see it happen in person."

"My family is coming to Paris?!"

"Your sister is coming Saturday. Originally, it was your entire family, but with the health of your grandmother we had to make some adjustments. She's staying at the Peninsula so she can be close to Fashion Week. I booked her a suite a long time ago. I figure we could stay there together"

"Hugh! Oh my gosh. Are you serious?"

"Yes, I'm serious. I hope that's okay."

"That's more than okay! I'm speechless. I don't know how I can thank you."

"I have an idea in mind. Let's set a date."

"For real?"

"I don't want to drag this out. I don't need years to plan a wedding. I love you. I just want to start our lives together."

"Okay, I can agree with that. Are you sure you don't want to think about this?"

"Of course we can think about it. We don't have to decide on this bridge. Let's go back to my flat and talk."

"I can't wait to be your wife."

"I love the sound of that."

# Twenty-Seven

## "Shine Bright Like a Diamond"

What the ring will look like has yet to cross my mind. On our cab ride home, the girls could not stop talking about our future wedding. Hugh and I just sit there and listen while he holds my hand in the backseat. I haven't even thought about my modeling ordeal since he proposed. All I can focus on is how I'm going to tell my parents. I want to call them right now. Actually, I think I will, considering it's a reasonable hour for them back in Charleston. I want to see the ring first, of course. I think we have an hour to spare before I make that call. I'm going to spend at least thirty minutes staring down at my finger once I get that ring on it!

We arrive to the flat and I don't even need to tell Addison and Claire that I'm staying with Hugh tonight. I tell them to give us five minutes alone and then I will come down to show them my ring. They beg me not to make them wait until the morning to see it. This night has had so many surprises that I can't even imagine what this surprise has in store. I don't even know what to picture in terms of an engagement ring. Hugh is so classy, yet so unpredictable. I'm shocked that he proposed in front of anyone. I never pictured placing a lock on the Lock Bridge that read "MARRY ME!" or that my sister was going to see it in person. I'm sure she's going to be shocked when I'm already wearing the ring when she sees us. I doubt she'll mind very much considering Hugh is spending so much to fly her out here and put her up in that incredibly swanky hotel.

After a long elevator ride to the sixth floor, we finally arrive to Hugh's flat. Once again, my heart is pounding in anticipation. I don't think my heart can handle much more or it will explode from too much excitement. Hugh picks me up and walks me through the threshold of his front door as if we're already married. I've never seen him quite this happy. I feel like he's been anticipating proposing for a long time now. After what happened in Monaco, I'm wondering if he had second thoughts about being engaged so soon into our relationship. I guess couples fight. That happens. I know we can't be perfect.

"Hold on. I need to get my safe so I can give you the ring," Hugh says as he reaches in the top of his closet for his little safe.

"No hurry. I'll just be sitting here envisioning my last name as Hamilton."

"I like the sound of that," Hugh says as he turns around with a little red box in his right hand.

Hugh is on one knee again, since he now has to re-propose, so it's like the first time.

"Scarlett Hanes, will you please do the honor of placing this diamond ring on your left hand?"

"YES."

I look down at the opened box, and I'm nearly blinded by how shiny it is. It's flawless. No pun intended. It's the most beautiful, emerald-cut ring I have ever seen. It's most definitely more than two carats. It has two small emerald diamonds on the side with a platinum band. Hugh places the ring on my left ring finger and looks me in the eye to tell me he loves me. He says he can't wait to spend the rest of his life with me. I look down at my hand and realize that this is what's been missing in my life. I truly feel whole now.

"Where did you find this incredible ring?"

"Cartier. On 5th avenue."

"When did you have time to do this without me knowing?"

"I have my ways, Scarlett. Don't you worry."

"It's perfect. It's truly perfect. I can't stop staring at it."

"You have a lifetime to stare at it. Give me some affection!"

"Of course!" Hugh nearly tackles me onto his bed. I totally forgot to go downstairs to show Addison and Claire because I was swept up in the heat of the moment.

I run downstairs to my flat to show Addison and Claire my ring. I can't wait to show this off to everyone in the world. It's so big and shiny. It fits my finger perfectly because Hugh took one of my rings to the jeweler to have it matched. He knew we would be in Paris and did not want to take any chances of it falling off. He had it insured before he left in case anything was to happen. I knock on the door and Addison and Claire are standing an inch from me in eagerness. I am so happy they are this excited for me.

"LET US SEE!"

"Okay, okay. Here it is!" I hold my left hand out and tilted my chin up to flaunt my ring.

"HOLY SMOKES. THIS THING IS HUGE!"

"He did a great job. He said he had it designed."

"Scarlett. You just hit the jackpot with Hugh."

"I feel like he hit the jackpot with me. Dontcha think?"

"HAHA, yes. I do. I'm so happy for you guys," Claire says as she pulls me in for a hug. Something I didn't expect. I guess I was so clouded by her thinking she liked Hugh that I couldn't see that it was just her trying to be a good friend.

"Thanks, Claire! I can't wait to have you and Addison stand by my side at my wedding." I can't believe I just said *my* wedding. I don't know how to feel about that word. It's such a crazy thing – thinking about getting married so soon and so young. It has me worried already. I know I shouldn't be worried since Hugh is older and more mature. I know he's ready. I'm ready, too. I love him and can't imagine my life with anybody but Hugh.

"Are you going to get married back home or in Australia?" Addison asks.

"I've never been to Australia. I imagine I'll get married in Charleston. That's where all my family is."

"What if Hugh doesn't accept that?" Claire chimes in.

"I'm sure he will. Hugh will pay to fly his family to our wedding. I'm sure he will rent a big house for them to stay in. We're getting ahead of ourselves."

"He said he wanted to set a date though. I'm sure he's thinking ahead," Addison says.

"We will set a date when my sister arrives. We already decided. I need to talk to my family. I haven't even called to tell them yet!"

"You should go back to Hugh and call your parents right now!" Addison excitedly says.

"Okay, you girls need to get some sleep since you're leaving in the morning for Switzerland."

"Okay! Goodnight, Mrs. Hamilton," they both say at once.

# Twenty-Eight
## Exhale

I walk back upstairs to Hugh's flat and realize it's nearly four in the morning. I have to be back at work in the morning to set up for the day. I know my adrenaline won't allow me to sleep. It's only ten at night back at home, so I figure it's the perfect time to call my parents. Hugh and I decide it would be more fun to FaceTime them to show them the ring. I would love to call my grandparents, but I know they won't be awake.

"Mom! Is this a good time to talk? Where are you?" I ask with Hugh sitting right next to me on the bed.

"Scarlett, I'm at the MUSC. Your grandmother is very sick. I didn't want to call you in the middle of the night to alarm you."

"What? Oh my gosh! Is she okay? What's going on?"

"The breast cancer has spread to her lungs. She can barely speak. The doctors don't think she has much longer."

"WHAT! Why didn't anyone tell me? Why am I just now finding out?"

"We knew you would want to come home if you knew."

"You're damn right I want to come home. How could you keep this from me!"

"Scarlett. I'm very fragile right now. Please, don't be upset with me."

"I'm so sorry, Ms. Riley," Hugh chimes in.

"Mom, I know this isn't the best time to share this, but we're calling to tell you that we're engaged!"

"Oh my gosh! Let me see the ring!"

I held my hand up to the screen to show my mom the ring. I feel like my amazingly perfect night has just crashed down on me into a million little pieces. I don't know what to do now. I'm trying not to let it ruin my night, as selfish as that sounds, but this is a memory I want to cherish forever.

"Scarlett, your sister isn't coming on Saturday. She doesn't want to leave right now. I'm so excited for you two. I hope you're able to celebrate despite the news of your grandmother."

"I'm coming home." Hugh looks at me like I'm crazy, but he gets it. "I can't stay here knowing she could die at any second and I won't be there to say goodbye. I know my family needs me.

"You can't come home. Fashion Week just started and that's why you're there."

"Fashion Week means nothing to me without my family. I'm coming home today and that's the end of that discussion."

"Ms. Riley, I will make sure Scarlett is home to be with you. I would come if I were able to. Thankfully, we will be family soon and I won't have to miss out on these kind of things."

"Thank you, Hugh, for everything you have done for my little girl. We can't wait to have you formally join our family. Scarlett is a lucky girl."

"Mom, I'll see you tomorrow. I'm so sorry you're going through this right now. Stay strong."

We were having the best night of our lives when the worst thing imaginable could have happened. There's nothing more important in my life than my family. I had the most incredible experience at Fashion Week last night and got engaged to the love of my life. What more could I want? I haven't even thought of what Courtney will say when I tell her I have to leave at the very beginning of Fashion Week. She's going to fire me. I'm sure of it. She will say that family is not more important than Paris Fashion Week. She will say that I have to make a choice. I don't care. I don't care what she says. She can fire me if she wants. I'm not going to miss the opportunity to be with my family and see my grandmother before she passes away. I pray she can pull through, but it doesn't sound promising.

Hugh holds me closer tonight as we fall asleep. He booked a flight for me to leave at eleven this morning. I'll have a car take me to Charles De Gaulle so I don't risk missing my flight. I'm so sad that I have to leave Hugh as soon as we get engaged, but he'll be flying to Charleston in a week to be with me as soon as Fashion Week is over. My time here was almost over anyways. I pray that my grandmother can wait another day and hang on so I can see her. All that's running through my mind are the many wonderful memories we've had together. I can't help but cry myself to sleep. I'm so heartbroken that this is happening right now. It's amazing how fast things can change for someone. In the blink of an eye it's all over. The fairytale has to come to an end at some point. I'm just hoping my fairytale has just begun.

I run downstairs to talk to Addison and Claire before my flight to tell them what's going on and to say my goodbyes to them. Addison and Claire have known my grandmother for years. They're so upset, and it's hard to say goodbye on these terms, but we must go. I can't be late for my flight since my connecting flight only has an hour in between. I wish I had more time to say goodbye to Paris. I wanted to do a few more things before I left the most beautiful city I have ever been to. Hugh and I had so many plans to travel around after Fashion Week was over. I know that everything happens for a reason, but I'm so sad thinking about my circumstances. It's hard leaving on this sad of a note, but I know I'll come back one day.

# Twenty-Nine
## Au Revoir

*Good Morning, Courtney –*

*It's with great sadness that I share with you today I have to depart from Paris to go home to Charleston. My grandmother is dying, and I need to be with my family during this difficult time.*

*I was able to secure an exclusive interview before the Marc Jacobs show with Naomi Campbell. I know you're probably going to be very upset that I can't stay to work the rest of the week, but family comes first. I'm sure you'll see photos or hear about it, so I'll go ahead and say that I ended up on the runway as a model for the Givenchy show. I'd say I'm sorry, but I'm not. Last night was the best night of my life. Hugh Hamilton asked me to marry him, and I said yes. Despite the great sadness I have regarding my grandmother's health, I will never forget the incredible opportunity you gave me to come to Paris and have this experience.*

*I understand if you have to let me go because of this, but just know I'm thankful for the time I was here.*

*Sincerely,*
*Scarlett*

After sending my email to Courtney, I text Hugh to let him know I was about to take off for Charleston. My seat is in first class, which is nice, and the lady beside me has been talking to me throughout the flight since I haven't been able to sleep. She reassured me that I was doing the right thing by going home to be with my family. I don't doubt my decision; I just wish I could have spent one more day with Hugh as a newly engaged couple. I'm sad that we had to leave like that this morning. I'm praying that my grandmother can pull through this. Sometimes the doctors are wrong. Sometimes they give worst-case scenarios to make sure they aren't promising something they can't follow through with on their end.

I only have an hour on this flight from Charlotte to Charleston. I feel my body giving out as I try to stand up to put my bag in the overhead compartment. I know I need to rest. I sit down, fasten my seatbelt, and close my eyes. I finally fall asleep. I have run out of tears to cry and my heart is completely shattered on the floor. I have never felt this kind of sadness before. I can't imagine what my mom is going through, or my grandfather. My sister is probably devastated that she had to cancel her trip to Paris, but I'm sure she'll get over it. As the plane to Charleston takes off, I quickly drift into a deep sleep.

•••

That flight felt like the fastest hour of my life. Instead of waking up refreshed, I feel like a zombie. It's nice to hear people speaking English all around me. I'm actually very glad to be home. I haven't been home since Christmas. I have such wonderful memories of baking pies back during the holidays with my grandmother and my mom. I'm going to cling to those memories as I step into the hospital this afternoon. The jetlag is going to creep up and hit me in an hour or two, I know it. I hear it's easier to acclimate when you come home. Right now, I feel pretty alert. Hungry, but alert.

I make my way down to baggage claim to get my very large suitcases from the conveyer belt. I look around and I don't see my mom. I pull my cell phone from my back pocket to see that my dad has text me. I look over my shoulder and see that he's standing near the door. I start balling my eyes out and run towards him. I have never felt happier to see family in my life. I'm so happy that my dad is the one to pick me up instead of my mom. I know she sent him for a reason – mostly because she can't leave her mom's side right now, but mainly because he's my rock. I keep thinking about what I'm going to say to everyone. My grandfather must be in shambles. I can't wait to hug his neck.

"How's my sweetheart?" my dad asks.

"I've seen better days, dad."

"I know, darlin. Everything is going to be fine. I'm so happy to see you. It feels like it's been forever."

"Yes, it sure does."

"I know you probably want to shower, but I think we should head straight to the hospital."

"Absolutely. I don't care about showering." I don't think I've ever said that in my life. It's funny how circumstances can change your once important needs or wants. "I have a change of clothes in my bag that I can slip on when I get there."

"Great. She can't have visitors past a certain time, so we better hurry."

We left the airport as soon as my other luggage arrived. It is almost rush hour traffic time in Charleston, so I'm hoping we beat this road congestion in order to see my grandmother in time. I'm so anxious, and I feel like we are moving so slowly. I need us to go faster! Luckily, my dad is coming in handy with his cop car, once again, to get me some place much faster than usual. I think it's appropriate during a time like this.

I check my emails on the way over to distract myself from the fact that we are stuck on the Cooper River Bridge right now. Getting downtown at this time of day should be much easier considering we have a siren on. You can't get around people on a bridge, unfortunately. To my surprise, I have an email from Courtney that I must have received as I was flying home.

*Dear Scarlett,*

*I'm so sorry to hear that your grandmother is not doing well. I completely understand that you had to leave Paris. As for your job, I wouldn't worry about it right now. Just be with your family. As for modeling the Givenchy show – kudos. Naomi Campbell? KUDOS.*

*Take Care,*
*Courtney*

I don't really know how to take the "As for your job, I wouldn't worry about it right now" statement. I feel like if my job was not in hot water she would just tell me. I feel like that's the most cryptic way of *not* telling me where my future stands with the company. She could've just been like, "Your job is just fine, Scarlett." But no! She had to put her selfish little manager tactics in her email. I'm glad she approved of the other stuff, but I feel like I'm going to be let go or demoted. I would reply to her, but that would insinuate that I'm not busy being with my family. I'm just going to do what she said and be with my family. I'm going to worry about myself right now. Hugh told me not to worry about *Cosmo*. He has a ton of connections in the magazine world, and he'll make sure his fiancé is taken care of!

My dad and I finally arrive at Medical University of South Carolina where my grandmother is receiving her treatment. I've been told that she's in the intensive care unit for cancer patients. I'm sure she's receiving the best care possible considering my grandparents have an entire wing named after them. My grandparents have always donated to the hospital because of my grandfather's involvement with veterans.

We walk through the doors of the hospital and I immediately panic. I start sweating and my heart is pounding. I can't imagine how sad I'm about to be when I see my family. I don't want to see my mom this sad. Or my sister. I worry about my grandfather and what he will do if he has to live alone. All of these things have been playing over and over in my head. How's it going to be when she's gone? I don't want to fathom the pain we are all about to endure. I try to wipe the tears off my face to be strong for my mom. I know she needs me to be strong right now. We head to the elevator and push the button for the 22nd floor. My dad has spent the last week visiting between his shifts at work. Despite the fact that my parents are divorced, they are still family, and Savannah and I need both of our parents right now.

We walk down the brightly lit hallway with the fluorescent lights beaming over our heads and the smell of hand sanitizer is stinging my eyes. I look around hoping to see my family. My dad thinks they may have left to grab some dinner. He points at her room and I run towards it leaving him behind. I quietly open the door to see that my grandmother is hooked up to every tube in the room. My heart sinks.

"Oh my gosh. Grandmother. I'm here!" I whisper as I sit down in the chair beside her.

I don't get a response out of her because she appears to be sleeping. I just lay my head down beside her and cry. I can't even feel anything right now because I'm so numb. I have never felt this way before and I really hope I don't have to for long. My dad tells me he is going to run and get some coffee downstairs. I hold my grandmother's hand carefully trying not to hurt her since she has an IV running through the top part of her hand. I just want to embrace her while she tells me it's going to be okay. I shouldn't have to be consoled by her. I should be the one telling her it will be okay. I've never had to be the one that's there for her. She's always been the one to make me feel better when I'm sad or hurting.

I didn't think I had more tears to cry, but when my grandmother whispered she loved me, I lost it.

"You're awake!"

"Yes, darling. I'm here," she whispers.

"I love you, too! So much! Oh my gosh. Why didn't anyone tell me how sick you were? I would have been here sooner!"

"Just lay here with me. Too weak to explain."

"Of course."

I got up on the bed to lie beside her. She held my hand and I brushed her hair out of her face. I'm having such a hard time sucking down my sadness and my tears. I've never seen her this weak before. I just wish I had known she was so sick. I might not have ever experienced Fashion Week or getting engaged had I known. Maybe my parents were waiting until Saturday to tell me. I could have missed her had they waited. I'm sure they knew it was risky. I don't know if I'd ever forgive them had they waited and she passed away.

"Hugh asked me to marry him in Paris last night. It was so romantic. You would have loved seeing it happen."

"The ring," she says quietly.

"Here it is. Isn't it beautiful?"

She nods yes and gives a smile.

I've been waiting all day to see her smile. It was worth leaving Paris just to see her smile again. I can't imagine not seeing her smile ever again.

"Scarlett, I want you to take care of your grandfather. He's not well."

"What?! He's sick too?!" I pop up out of bed. I told her I would be right back. I had to look for my dad or the doctor to ask what was going on.

I'm furious with my family right now. I can't believe they have been holding out on me and not telling me my grandparents are BOTH sick. The tables have turned, and they are now the ones lying to me. Being deceptive and keeping things from me is one thing, but straight up lying and not telling me is another. I'm so upset right now I just want to scream.

"DAD!" I yell out from halfway down the hallway.

"You can't scream in here, miss," one of the nurses exclaims. I walked down the hall as fast as I could to get to my dad.

"Grandfather is sick, too!?" I yell at him.

"I know you're going to be upset, but your mother wouldn't let me tell you."

"What is wrong with you people? I need to know these things!" Maybe this is what Courtney meant when she told me not to worry about my job. My job is the last thing I'm worried about now, or ever. I only care about the well being of my family.

"He's okay, Scarlett. He had a major heart attack when you were in Monaco. Your mother wanted to tell you, but she knew you would be on the next flight out."

"You're damn right I would. I'm not happy with y'all right now."

"I know, sweetie. I'm sorry. He's okay though. He had bypass surgery and he's fine. He's resting at home and has a nurse watching him at all times. He'll be here in the morning to see your grandmother."

"I want to see him tonight!"

"He's resting. You can see him in the morning."

"What if I lose both of them and I only get to say goodbye to one?"

"He's much stronger than you think. He's going to be just fine. The doctors have said he's better now than he was."

"I'm still mad. I can't believe nobody told me."

"You might not have that ring on your finger if we had."

"I don't care about a stupid ring! I care about my family!"

"Well, that's good to know!" my dad laughs and pulls me in for a hug. I can't stay mad at him for too long. I guess parents always know best.

# Thirty

## September 9th

I sat by my grandmother's bedside all night. I didn't even eat dinner or wash my face. I just fell into a deep sleep. I had a dream that everything was fine and we were all in Paris drinking red wine and watching the sunset together by the Eiffel Tower. That's what was supposed to happen this weekend. I still can't believe nobody told me my grandparents were this sick. I guess everything happens the way it's supposed to. I look down at my hand and think about the best night of my life – the happiness I felt when Hugh asked me to marry him. I'm still in awe that he asked me so soon in our relationship, but I'm happy considering life is so short. I don't want to waste time with a long engagement. I want to marry Hugh as soon as I can.

"Hey, babe. I know it's really late there, but I couldn't stop thinking about you. I'm sorry if I woke you up."

"Hey, love. How are you?" Hugh asks in a quiet voice as if I had actually woke him up.

"Do you want to talk later after you get some sleep?"

"No, now is good. What's up?"

"I was just thinking about September."

"What about September?"

"I was thinking we should get married in September."

"Really? You would have a six month engagement?"

"Yes. Absolutely."

"September sounds perfect."

"I thought I'd let you pick the date."

"How about 9-9-2017"

"That sounds great. I like the cadence."

"I'll tell my family. I know you haven't met them yet, but I thought I could fly us to Australia once things calm down at home for you."

"Really? That sounds amazing. I've never been. And of course I want to meet your family!"

"Great. We will work on that when I'm in Charleston next weekend."

"I can't wait to see you. You've already put a smile on my face."

"I'm so glad. I love you more than anything, Scarlett."

"Me too. I'm so happy I get to be your wife."

He always knows the perfect way to calm my nerves and bring me back down to Earth. I really don't know how I got so lucky with Hugh. September doesn't seem very far away, but if this has taught me anything, it's that you don't get second chances often. We could have easily broken up back at Christmas, but we didn't. I think we can get through anything if we can get through what I put him through with my lying. I still feel bad that we started a relationship based off a lie, but I'm so glad that it brought us together the way it did.

It's nearly seven in the morning and I haven't slept very well since Wednesday night. I need to go home and shower, but I know my family will be arriving soon. I make my way back to my grandmother's room and see that my dad is holding her hand. This totally melts my heart. They haven't had the best relationship over the years, but I know they love each other. It's times like this that truly show someone how you feel. You might not ever get the chance to tell someone goodbye if you don't take the opportunity to. My dad has never said anything foul about my mom's family. *Not once.* He's always been a gentleman about things. I know he cheated on my mom, but that doesn't have anything to do with his relationship with them. Sure, he disrespected their daughter and things fell apart. Nobody is perfect. I'm just happy to see him being so sweet and loving to her.

I step outside the room to call my mom to find out when she and Savannah will be joining us. She says it will be another hour or two considering she has to go by grandfather's to pick him up and bring him. I told her I would come over there now, take a shower, and ride back with them. I'm so eager to see my grandfather. Frankly, I'm torn as to which grandparent I need to be with more right now. I guess if I don't take care of myself and sneak in a shower, I won't be worth very much to either of them.

So that my dad wouldn't have to leave my grandmother alone, I'm having an Uber take me to my grandparent's house. I wasn't very far from their house, so I decide that plan would be easiest for everyone. I'm anxious to see everyone and also see the condition he's in. I have to hope that he's doing much better than I expect. Surely they wouldn't lie to me that much.

# Thirty-One
## "It's Never Easy to Say Goodbye"

The weekend passed and I knew it would be hard, but not this hard. Sunday night, at 10:34 p.m., my grandmother, Lucy Riley, died. I'm so numb I don't even know how to explain this pain. My grandfather has never been this sad and I've never seen my mom cry so much. I'm lucky to have my grandfather, but I'm worried that his health won't hold up now that he is alone. I still can't believe she's gone. We were all able to have a great last night with her on Saturday. She was not well on Sunday, so the doctors knew she did not have much time left. It was hard to watch her suffer yesterday. On Saturday, we were able to get a few laughs out of her, and she told us something kind of bizarre.

"I want you all to think of me when I'm gone. Whenever you see a pink bird, think of me," she said.

We all looked at each other in bewilderment. Funny thing about pink flamingos these days is that they are all over. I will never stop thinking about my grandmother. I don't need to see a pink bird to remember her. I will never forget Lucy Riley. I'm so blessed I was able to spend a few more days with her and my family. I will never forget the time we had, laughing and crying, holding her hand, and kissing her forehead goodbye. My grandfather is going to need me now more than ever. I don't see how I can go back to New York and work. I don't know that I want to. If the doctor told me he only had six months to live, I would not move back. I couldn't do that to him. Hugh will be here on Wednesday night, and the funeral is Thursday morning. I hate that he had to cut his trip so short, but I need him so much right now. I know we're all glad that my grandmother isn't suffering anymore, but I'm so sad she's not here with us. It still doesn't feel real. I know it won't hit me for weeks that she isn't here. With Mother's Day coming up in a couple of months, I'm sure it will be really hard on all of us.

"Mom, is there anything I can do for you?"

"No, honey. Just come lay in here and watch a movie with me and your sister."

"Okay. I can do that." I walk in the room and lay in the middle with them. "How are you so strong, mom?"

"My mom taught me to be strong. Just like I've taught you girls."

"I guess you're right. I guess we are pretty tough," Savannah says.

"She'd want us to be happy. She wouldn't want us to be sad right now. She wants us to keep living and to live well."

"You're right."

"She'd want us to plan the most beautiful wedding EVER!" my mom says as she puts my hair behind my ear.

"I'm sad she won't be there to watch me walk down the aisle."

"What are you talking about? Of course she'll be there!"

"I guess that's true. Maybe I can have a song played in her memory."

"She'd rather you play a fun song at your reception and dance with your grandfather. She wouldn't want to be remembered that way. She was fun and free-spirited."

"Yep, she sure was. I remember the time she pulled me out of high school to take me shopping and to the movies. It was out of nowhere. Just a random Wednesday afternoon."

"Yeah, she did that with me one time, too," Savannah says.

"She was wonderful. I had a great relationship with my mom. I'm so happy God chose her to be my mom and that he chose you girls to be my daughters."

We spent most of the afternoon distracting ourselves by planning ideas for my wedding with Hugh. My grandmother didn't want a big funeral with a lot of people there. She wanted just family and for us to go out on grandfather's boat to spread her ashes in the ocean. She said she felt happiest when she was riding the boat with all of us. We decide it's best to honor her wishes. We know that she would be sad if we didn't. So, we took the afternoon to ride on the boat. Thankfully, the doctor cleared my grandfather to go. I was able to drive the boat for us, which worked out nicely. On our way back from spreading her ashes, we saw a pink flamingo float on the dock of someone's house. I knew it was a sign from my grandmother that she was with us in spirit. I'm glad she was able to tell us how she wanted us to remember her.

•••

The next couple of days passed and Hugh and I were finally able to sit down and talk about our future together – the fun part of being engaged and planning a wedding. The only issue we came across was my job. Courtney didn't fire me, but I had wondered if I really wanted to move back to the city. I have always said that I would never live in New York City, permanently. Hugh has mentioned the idea of moving away from NYC, but I wasn't sure he was ready to make a permanent move. I have a feeling he's going to be ready to start a family shortly after our nuptials. Something I'm not totally opposed to, honestly.

With all that has happened, and the fact that my grandfather is not in his healthiest state, I really want to consider my options. It's something I don't have to decide right this second, but I do need to figure things out soon.

Hugh and I have a big six months ahead of us. I never thought I'd be getting married at such a young age. I always thought I'd be in my thirties and find someone through online dating. I guess I underestimated myself big time. It's possible I should make this official before I lose my chances.

"Hugh, how would you feel about making this official sooner than September?"

"What are you saying, Scarlett?"

"You know exactly what I'm alluding to."

"Your family would kill us."

"What do you mean? They love you!"

"They also love YOU. They've been planning your fairytale wedding since you were born. You cannot deny them of that after everything that's happened with your family lately."

"If Lucy Riley could give me one *last* piece of advice, I know she would say life is short-marry Hugh today…"

# Acknowledgements

When I started writing *Pink Lies in Paris*, I knew that my personal experiences living overseas would impact the storyline. It's true that a lot of fiction comes from a real place. A lot of people ask me if I write from a real place, and I tell them, of course! A lot of the places you went in this book were places that I've been to or things that I've done. I will never forget the Fat Tire Bike Tour that my mom and I went on in Paris where we met Miss Brazil, and we did go to the Irish Pub afterwards, too. I'll always cherish those memories we had.

I think it goes without saying that I'm thankful to my friends and my family for supporting me as an author. I thank my husband, Marcus, for sharing his experience in France with me as he played basketball there. I'm so fortunate that I was able to live overseas and have such a rich experience. I'll never forget the times we had in Europe.

A huge bit of gratitude goes to my incredibly talented editor, Laci Swann, of Sharp Editorial. I don't know what I would do without you, and I'm so blessed you decided to help me on my journey to become a better author. Your benevolence has shown me that there are truly great people in this world, and I'm so happy I have you as my editor. You've been a wonderful cheerleader to me when I have been faced with writer's block. I'm excited to see where the next installment of *Pink Lies* is headed with your help and your direction!

Thank you to all of my readers who praise my work and make me realize that all the hard work and countless hours of writing is for a reason. You are the reason. Thank you for taking the time to read my novels and for your continued support throughout my journey.

I love you all so very much!

# About the Author

Haley Kitts graduated from East Carolina University with a B.S. in Communication and Public Relations where she developed a love for words and writing. She then spent time abroad in France eating croissants and drinking espresso while watching her husband play professional basketball. She loves watching Ina Garten & Bobby Flay and cooking the marvelous food they share on their shows. Haley lives in Raleigh, North Carolina, where she grew up visiting Wrightsville Beach many times – playing in the sand, surfing, wakeboarding, and eventually getting married there in 2014. Haley's freshmen effort, *Pink Lies*, is now a two-part series; soon to be three. Keep reading to find out what happens with Scarlett and her big wedding this September!

Website: www.haleytoddkitts.com
Facebook: www.facebook.com/HaleyToddKittsAuthor
Instagram: www.instagram.com/label_me_hales/

Made in the USA
Columbia, SC
24 February 2019